Tally the Stars

Tally the Stars

Lights of the Collapse
Book 3

Millie Copper

Written by Millie Copper

Edited by Ameryn Tucker

Proofread by MDC Proofreading

Cover design by Dauntless Cover Design

Also by Millie Copper

The Havoc in Wyoming Series

When a series of coordinated attacks devastate the United States, the people of Bakerville, Wyoming, must come together to survive. Unfortunately, not everyone has the town's best interest at heart. Some are striving for personal gain during the apocalypse.

The Montana Mayhem Series

A group from Bakerville, Wyoming strikes out on their own while searching for the desires of their heart. Unfortunately, the road will not be easy, and sometimes the heart is hardened and deceitful. When things don't work out as they hoped, will they become stranded in the wilderness? Or will each be able to find their way home?

The Dakota Destruction Series

After a series of coordinated attacks devastate the United States, Katie and Leo sacrifice everything to help their country. But some things aren't as they seem. Is it time to go home and start fresh, or can something good come out of this terrible situation?

In The October Fall World

In the blink of an eye, an EMP changed everything for Lauren and her family. Now they are in a fight for survival, trying to keep their loved ones alive as society collapses around them. Their once peaceful town of Cody, Wyoming has turned into a powder keg. And with law enforcement a thing of the past, evil lurks around every corner.

Nonfiction Books

Millie has penned seven nonfiction, traditional food focused books, sharing how, with a little creativity, anyone can transition to a real foods diet without overwhelming their food budget. Many of her books also include preparedness and food storage tips.

Find these titles at:
MillieCopper.com

Join My Reader's Club!

Receive a complimentary copy of *Starborn: A Lights of the Collapse Short Story Prequel.* As part of my reader's club, you'll be the first to know about new releases and specials. I also share info on books I'm reading, preparedness tips, and more. Please sign up at:

MillieCopper.com/Freebie

Chapter 1

The antiseptic scent of the doctor's office waiting room made Kaelyn's stomach curl. Or maybe it was the dull ache in her arm, a constant reminder of her clumsiness. She shifted in the hard plastic chair, trying to find a position where the throbbing would subside and the queasiness might ease.

Her grandmother, Joyce, sat beside her, flipping through a well-worn magazine. The doctor was running behind schedule, and Kaelyn had grown restless. An elderly man dozed in the corner, his chin tucked against his chest, his leg in a walking cast. A woman in a flowy summer dress held her phone in one hand while her other arm, like Kaelyn's, rested in a sling.

A row of planters divided the waiting room. Beyond them, she could see the tops of several people's heads. The soft hum of the air conditioner filled the space, punctuated by the occasional rustle of paper or gentle tapping on the receptionist's keyboard.

She wished she had brought a notebook so she could jot down some story ideas. Since she was stuck in Cody for the summer, she'd decided she was going to finally finish one of the many stories she had in progress.

A soft ding broke the quiet. She glanced over to see her grandma pulling out her phone, a smile spreading across her face as she read the message.

"It's your parents," Grandma Joyce said, her voice warm with affection. "They've arrived. They'll rest in the hotel today, then they'll be taken to the building site tomorrow."

"Okay," Kaelyn responded, unable to keep the lack of enthusiasm from her voice. She stared down at her sling, wishing she could disappear into it.

Grandma Joyce sighed and slipped her phone back into her purse. "I know this isn't how you planned to spend your summer— "

"It's fine, Grandma," Kaelyn cut her off, not wanting to rehash the conversation they'd had dozens of times already.

"No, it's not fine," her grandmother persisted, her tone gentle but firm. "You and your family had plans."

Frustration bubbled up inside Kaelyn. "Until I tripped over my own shoelace and ruined everything. At least my parents still get to do what we planned."

"It wasn't your shoelace. Your dad says you didn't see the stump. Hiking along as happily as could be and *bam*. The next thing they knew, you were on the ground."

"Humph. Then why was my shoe untied?" she muttered. She didn't bother correcting her grandma about her supposed happiness. She hadn't wanted to go hiking, but her parents insisted. They said the exercise would do her good and help prepare her for the long days of work ahead over the summer. So much for that.

"They wanted to stay home with you," her grandma continued. "Make sure you were fine. Your grandpa and I thought . . . we thought us taking care of you would be okay with you."

Kaelyn sighed, a sound that seemed to come from the depths of her being. She turned to her grandmother, noting the concern written across her features. "It is okay. I'm just . . . my arm hurts, and I'm worried about what the doctor is going to say. I've already ruined my summer. What if it ruins my senior year of high school too?"

Grandma Joyce's expression softened. "They'll say you are healing well. It's been almost two weeks since the surgery. I'm sure it's going to be fine. Besides, I think if there was any concern, you'd be seeing Dr. Newton and not his associate."

"I guess," Kaelyn murmured.

"I know you're upset that you're missing out on this. Africa was important to you. It was your start."

"My start?"

"Yes, the start you thought might help you change the world."

"I didn't think I could change the world. I just wanted to help build the school."

"That's how the world *is* changed. To you, it was just building a school, but it's more to those who need the school." Grandma Joyce smiled at her, warmth shining in her eyes.

The front door to the waiting room swung open. While her grandma grabbed a magazine, Kaelyn's attention was caught by a young man on crutches as he entered the room, likely just a few years older than her. He flashed a quick smile in her direction as he went to the reception desk. A rush of warmth spread across Kaelyn's cheeks, and she quickly dropped her gaze. She awkwardly ran her hand through her hair, smoothing it.

"I sure hope the wait isn't much longer," Grandma Joyce muttered as she flipped a page. "We're supposed to meet your grandpa for lunch at the Irma at one o'clock."

Instead of replying, Kaelyn stole a glance at the man on crutches, watching him discreetly through her lashes. Once he finished checking in, he scanned the waiting area. When his gaze landed on Kaelyn, he smiled again and made his way to the row of chairs across from her and her grandmother.

He was cute, in a rugged sort of way, with tousled brown hair and a strong jawline. He seemed nice, too, offering smiles as he passed. He wouldn't be interested in her. She was probably four or five years younger than him, and definitely not his type. She knew she wasn't pretty. Too tall and gangly, with a long nose and hair that never cooperated. When he leaned forward to grab a magazine from the table, the gun holstered at his hip caught her attention.

Guns were a common sight in Cody, Wyoming. People open carried on the street, in grocery stores, and even in church. But in a doctor's office? That was strange, even for Cody. Then again, with all the bizarre stuff happening lately, maybe it wasn't strange at all.

Over the past few weeks, the news had been flooded with wild stories. Unusual events seemed to be cropping up everywhere, or maybe they were easier to notice now with the internet, social media, and the relentless twenty-four-hour news cycle.

That was something she and her folks had been looking forward to. While they would have internet and cell service in East Africa, at least to a point, they'd be so busy helping build a school that they wouldn't have time to surf the web much for the eight weeks they were there.

As Kaelyn pondered this, she noticed the young man's demeanor change. His eyes, which had been alert and friendly moments ago, now seemed distant and unfocused. Magazine in hand, he stared off into space, his gaze fixed on a point somewhere over her shoulder.

A low, melodic hum began to fill the air. It took Kaelyn a moment to realize it was coming from him. The tune was vaguely familiar, but she couldn't quite place it. The humming grew louder, drawing curious and concerned looks from other patients.

"Kaelyn Fisher?" a nurse called out, her voice cutting through the strange tension that had settled over the waiting room.

Kaelyn startled, her eyes snapping away from the humming man. "That's me," she said, though her voice sounded off, too high and uncertain.

As she stood, her bag caught on the armrest of the chair. She tugged it free, only for the strap to slip through her fingers and the bag to tumble to the floor with a dull thud. Flustered, she quickly bent to grab it, her face hot with embarrassment.

The young man blinked rapidly, as if coming back to himself, and gave her a nod and a disarming smile. Kaelyn sighed under her breath and hurried after the nurse, with Grandma Joyce trailing behind.

In the examination room, the nurse, an older woman with graying hair and tired eyes, went through the motions of checking Kaelyn's vitals. Her tone was brisk but kind.

"How's the pain been?" the nurse asked as she examined her arm.

"It hurts sometimes," she admitted. "But the pills seem to help."

"Are you still using the prescription you got after the surgery?"

As she shook her head, Grandma Joyce said, "Not the narcotic. She only took those for the first couple of days. Only acetaminophen since."

The nurse nodded and made a note in her chart. "That's good. The doctor will be in shortly to— "

Her words were cut off by a piercing scream from somewhere in the building. The nurse froze, her eyes wide with shock. Another scream followed before Kaelyn heard the unmistakable sound of gunfire.

"What on earth?" the nurse whispered, her professional demeanor cracking. She rushed to the door, locking it with trembling hands. "We've had active shooter training," she said, her voice shaky but determined. "Get behind the counter or the bed. Now!"

Kaelyn's movements slowed, as if she were wading through molasses, as she stumbled off the examination table.

"Hurry, now!" Her grandmother gripped her good arm, helping her duck behind the table. They huddled together, Kaelyn's heart pounding so hard she was sure it would burst from her chest. The nurse crouched behind the counter. Her breathing was labored, and her face was pale.

More gunshots rang out, closer this time. Kaelyn could hear the sound of running feet in the hallway. She buried her face in her grandmother's shoulder, trying to block out the terrifying noises.

"It's okay, sweetheart," Grandma Joyce murmured, stroking Kaelyn's hair. "We're going to be okay." She did not sound convinced.

Time seemed to stretch endlessly as they waited in tense silence. Kaelyn's arm throbbed, the pain intensified by fear and adrenaline. She focused on her breathing, trying to stay calm.

After what seemed like hours but was probably only minutes, they heard new sounds. The wail of police sirens, shouted commands, and the thud of heavy boots echoed in the hallway.

A sharp knock on the door made them all jump. "Police! Is anyone in there?"

The nurse peered out cautiously from behind the table. "Yes, we're here. Three of us. We're fine. I've locked the door."

"Stay where you are. We'll be back for you."

Kaelyn relaxed slightly at the sound of the officer's voice. She glanced at her grandmother, who gave her a small, reassuring nod. The nurse let out a shaky breath.

"Do you think it's over?" Kaelyn whispered to her grandmother.

"I hope so, dear," she replied softly. "But let's stay quiet for now, just in case."

Finally, they heard footsteps approaching again.

"Police," came the same voice from earlier. "We need you to unlock the door now. Once you've done that, step away from it."

The nurse quickly unlocked the door and stepped back. Two officers entered, their weapons drawn and eyes scanning the room.

"Is everyone all right?" one of the officers asked, his gaze softening as it fell on Kaelyn and her grandmother.

Grandma Joyce nodded and helped Kaelyn to her feet. "We're fine. What . . . what happened?"

The officer exchanged a glance with his partner before answering. "There was an incident in the waiting room. It's under control now. We need to get you all out of here for your safety."

As they were led out of the exam room, Kaelyn couldn't help but notice the grim expressions on the faces of the medical staff they passed. When they reached the waiting room, her breath caught in her throat. The space was in disarray, with toppled furniture and shattered glass on the reception desk.

Her eyes were fixated on two figures on the floor, covered with white sheets. Poking out from underneath one of the sheets was the bright fabric of a woman's sundress—the same pattern the woman in the sling had been wearing. She quickly looked away, her stomach churning.

"Ma'am." A police officer approached them, notepad in hand. "I need to ask you a few questions about what you saw."

Grandma Joyce nodded but kept a protective arm around Kaelyn's shoulders. "Of course, Officer."

As her grandmother recounted their experience, clarifying they were in the exam room when they heard the screams and shooting, Kaelyn's mind whirled. She caught snippets of conversations around her. Shocked whispers, tearful phone calls, and worried discussions about the state of the world.

"I can't believe this is happening in Cody," she heard a woman say, her voice trembling. "It's exactly like what we've been hearing about in other places."

"All this increased violence," an older man replied, shaking his head. "Never thought we'd see it here."

As they were finally cleared to leave, Kaelyn spotted a nurse talking to another officer. "He was here to get his leg checked. Seemed fine when he came in. Everything was normal. Until he started singing," the nurse said, her voice trembling. "All soft and sinister like. The next thing I knew, he was shooting."

"Singing? Singing what?" the officer pressed.

"I don't know. I-I wasn't paying attention. Not really. Not until the first shot was fired."

A sudden chill swept over Kaelyn as realization dawned on her. The shooter must have been the man who'd smiled at her in the waiting room. The cute guy on crutches. Deep down, she probably knew that when she first heard the gunshots. This was her fault. If she'd told someone about his gun . . .

Her eyes darted around the chaotic scene, searching for him. Where was he now? She couldn't spot him among the injured being treated, and a sinking feeling in her stomach told her he was probably dead.

Kaelyn and her grandmother were free to go after providing their contact information. As her grandmother led the way to the car, questions piled up in Kaelyn's head. Was this her fault? If she'd mentioned seeing the gun on his hip, would it have made a difference?

If she'd told her grandma, she'd have brushed her off. Grandma Joyce herself often carried a pistol, as did Grandpa Terry. Even her parents carried guns when the family went hiking. It was something smart to do when living in grizzly bear country.

"We should . . . we should probably go home instead of meeting your grandpa for lunch." Grandma Joyce checked the time. "Oh, we're already late, and you know as well as I do that he won't have his phone on him. We'll go to the restaurant and tell him. Once we're home, I'll make you a grilled cheese sandwich with tomato soup. Does that sound good?"

Kaelyn could only shrug.

As they drove downtown to the Irma in tense silence, Kaelyn watched the familiar streets of Cody. The town appeared untouched. Tourists still wandered the sidewalks, shops bustled with activity, and life carried on as always.

But for her, everything was different. The world had become a place of danger and uncertainty.

Chapter 2

The Irma Hotel's dining room buzzed with the usual lunchtime chatter when Kaelyn and her grandmother entered. The scent of grilled meat and fresh-baked bread filled the air, a stark contrast to the terrible smells of the doctor's office they'd just left. Kaelyn's arm throbbed dully in its sling, a constant reminder of the morning's traumatic events.

When would she be able to see the doctor? She'd been rushed out so quickly she didn't even know if her doctor was among the injured or when they might resume office visits.

Grandpa Terry waved them over to a table near the famous Cherrywood back bar, his weathered face creasing into a smile. Kaelyn focused on him, eager to escape her thoughts, but as she stepped forward, her foot skidded on a perfectly smooth patch of floor. She stumbled, lurching sideways, only to catch herself on the edge of a nearby chair.

The man sitting in it jolted and glanced up at her with a startled expression. "Whoa, there," he said, his tone light but his brow furrowing.

"Sorry," Kaelyn mumbled, her cheeks flushing. She straightened quickly and avoided his gaze.

"No problem," the man said, watching her closely. "Everything okay?"

Kaelyn forced a shaky smile and a nod. "Fine, thank you." She gave him an awkward wave with her good hand, grateful when Grandma Joyce gently urged her forward toward the table.

Grandpa Terry stood as they approached the table. "I've already ordered for you," he began, then paused, taking in their disheveled appearances and tense postures. "Figured the doctor— " He stopped again, his brow furrowing. "What's wrong?"

Kaelyn sank into a chair, feeling the weight of the morning's events pressing down on her. She reached for the water glass already in place. Her hand shook so hard as she lifted it to her mouth that some of it sloshed over the edge. The familiar surroundings of the Irma, a place that had always represented safety and comfort, now felt surreal after what she'd experienced.

Grandma Joyce motioned for him to sit. "Oh, Terry," she said, her voice barely above a whisper. "Something terrible has happened."

In hushed tones, she recounted the horrific events at the doctor's office. Kaelyn listened numbly as her grandmother spoke. The young man's friendly smile, the sound of his humming, the sudden destruction and terror that followed. It all swirled in her thoughts, making her feel dizzy and nauseous. The nagging feeling that she should've said something filled her with guilt.

Grandpa Terry's face paled as he listened, his grip on Grandma Joyce's hand tightening. "Oh no," he breathed, shaking his head in disbelief. "I saw the police go screaming by, but I had no idea. Are you both all right? Kaelyn, your arm— "

"It's fine," she mumbled, though the ache had intensified since their hasty exit from the doctor's office. She avoided her grandfather's concerned gaze, focusing instead on the intricate patterns of the tablecloth.

A woman at the next table, who had been unsubtly eavesdropping, leaned over. Her eyes were wide with curiosity and concern. "Did something happen? We heard sirens earlier, but no one seems to know anything."

Grandpa Terry hesitated, glancing at Kaelyn before responding. "Something happened at the orthopedics office," he said carefully. "A shooting."

The woman's hand flew to her mouth. "A shooting? Here in Cody?"

Her exclamation caught the attention of nearby diners, and soon the entire restaurant was abuzz with the news. Whispers and shocked voices rippled through the crowd, the peaceful lunch atmosphere shattered by the terrible reality of what had occurred mere blocks away.

"I can't believe it," a man at a nearby table said, shaking his head. "Cody's always been so safe."

"It's happening everywhere these days," his companion replied. "I guess we're not immune after all."

The waitress arrived with their food, her cheerful demeanor at odds with the somber mood that had settled over their table. She set down the plates, her smile faltering as she sensed the tension.

"Is everything all right?" she asked, looking from one distraught face to another.

Grandpa Terry nodded, forcing a small smile. "Yes, thank you. Some bad news, that's all."

Clicking her tongue, Grandma Joyce said, "Might as well tell her, Terry. Everyone else already knows."

As he quickly recounted the event, the waitress shook her head. "I can't believe it. I simply can't believe it."

As the waitress retreated, Grandpa Terry gestured at the plates. "Well, we might as well eat. No sense in letting good food go to waste."

"I'm not hungry," Kaelyn mumbled, her stomach still churning with guilt and shock. The events of the morning kept replaying in her mind.

"Please, try to eat," her grandfather urged, his voice gentle. "I ordered you the salmon salad you like so much. You need to keep up your strength."

Kaelyn looked down at the plate. The Bear Salad, as it was called, did look appetizing. A bed of crisp lettuce topped with plump blackberries, tart raspberries, crumbly feta cheese, and crunchy walnuts, all crowned with a perfectly grilled piece of salmon. Under normal circumstances, she would have dug in eagerly.

As her grandparents started on their meals—fish and chips for Grandma Joyce and a hearty burger for Grandpa Terry—Kaelyn picked at her salad. The only good thing about breaking her arm was she'd broken her right one. Since she was left-hand dominant, she was still able to write and hold a fork as usual.

The normalcy of the scene struck her as surreal. How could they sit here, eating lunch, when an hour ago people had died? When she had seen firsthand how quickly life could change, and how fragile their sense of safety actually was?

She forced herself to take a bite, the flavors barely registering as her mind continued to race. The restaurant around them hummed with conversation, most of it now centered on the shooting. Kaelyn caught snippets as she mechanically chewed her food.

". . . never thought it would happen here . . ."

". . . just like those incidents in the big cities . . ."

". . . what's the world coming to?"

Trying to distract herself, Kaelyn let her eyes wander to the Cherrywood back bar. Its intricate carvings and polished surface gleamed in the afternoon light, a testament to its storied history. She recalled the tale her grandpa had told her countless times about how the bar had been a gift to Buffalo Bill Cody from Queen Victoria herself in 1900, in gratitude for a command performance.

The bar's journey from France to Cody had been an epic tale in itself. Across the Atlantic by steamer, by rail to Montana, and finally by horse-drawn wagon to its current home. Now valued at over $100,000, it was more than a piece of furniture; it was a tangible link to Cody's vibrant past.

As Kaelyn's gaze traced the detailed woodwork, she found herself wondering about the people who had stood before the bar over the decades. How many of them had faced their own world-changing events? How had they coped with the uncertainty, the fear?

The conversations around them continued to ebb and flow. While some were still discussing the shooting, others had moved on to the broader troubles plaguing the country and the world.

"It's not only here," a man nearby said. "Have you been following the news? There have been so many of these random acts of violence lately. It's like the whole world's gone mad."

His companion nodded solemnly. "I heard about an incident in New York last week. And the one in Atlanta before that. It's almost like out of a horror movie."

The man chuckled nervously. "Pretty soon, we'll start having zombies."

A chill crawled down Kaelyn's spine at their words. She'd heard about those other incidents. The news was impossible to avoid. People had lost control and lashed out at those around them. A girl in a subway had taken a kitchen knife with her, using it on several people before she was stopped. Someone drove a truck into a crowd, something that'd been done many times in the past, but the driver was young, even younger than Kaelyn, and insisted he hadn't known what he was doing.

The stories were many, but she'd always thought of them as distant, disconnected from her life in quiet, safe Cody. Now, her illusion of safety had been shattered.

She was about to turn back to her salad when a busboy walked past their table. He was humming softly to himself as he collected dishes from a nearby table. "Twinkle, Twinkle, Little Star." She glanced at him, wondering why someone like him would be humming a children's tune.

Her breath caught, and her fork clattered onto the plate as she watched the guy walk away, oblivious to her reaction. She realized it was the same song the shooter had been humming in the waiting room.

"Kaelyn?" Grandma Joyce's voice cut through her rising panic. "Are you all right, dear? You've gone quite pale."

Kaelyn tore her gaze away from the retreating busboy, trying to calm her racing heart. "I'm fine," she managed, though her voice sounded strained even to her own ears. "Just thinking about what happened."

Her grandmother reached across the table and patted her hand gently. "I know it's hard, sweetheart. But we're safe now. Try not to dwell on it too much."

Kaelyn nodded, not trusting herself to speak. How could she explain the connection she'd made? Would they think she was overreacting, seeing threats where there were none? And yet, she couldn't shake the feeling something was very, very wrong. She should say something, tell her grandparents about what she suspected.

She pressed her lips together and took a breath, but Grandma Joyce was already telling Grandpa Terry about the text from Kaelyn's parents. She didn't want to interrupt, especially since the busboy had disappeared into the back. Everything seemed fine.

As they finished their meal, the waitress returned with a professional smile. "Did everything taste all right? Any room for dessert?"

Grandpa Terry leaned back and patted his round belly. "No, I couldn't eat another bite. Although I'm tempted by the bread pudding with whiskey sauce."

The waitress laughed. "It's one of our specialties. Are you sure I can't twist your arm?"

As Grandpa Terry shook his head, a man at the next table called out to the waitress. "Excuse me, miss? Do you smell that?"

The waitress turned, her brow furrowing. "Smell what, sir?"

"I'm not sure," the man said, sniffing the air. "It's like . . . Is it smoke? Or maybe gas?"

A woman at his table nodded in agreement. "I smell it too. It's getting stronger."

The waitress frowned and glanced toward the kitchen. "I'll go check with the kitchen staff. Perhaps something's burning."

As she hurried away, a sense of unease grew in the pit of Kaelyn's stomach. The busboy's song, and now this strange smell . . . it all seemed wrong, like pieces of a puzzle she couldn't quite fit together.

She was about to suggest to her grandparents that they leave when she was knocked from her chair. A deafening explosion rocked the building, sending her spiraling across the floor. Pain shot through her injured arm.

For a moment, all Kaelyn could hear was the high-pitched ringing in her ears. Smoke filled the air, making it hard to breathe. As her hearing slowly returned, she became aware of screams and the sound of shattering glass. Through the haze, she could make out figures stumbling about, some helping others, some lying motionless on the ground.

"Kaelyn!" Her grandmother's voice cut through the din, tight with fear. "Kaelyn, where are you? Are you all right?"

She struggled to her feet, coughing from the smoke. "I'm here, Grandma! I'm okay!"

She squinted through the confusion, finally spotting her grandparents a few feet away. They were both on the ground, looking shaken but largely unharmed. Grandpa Terry had a cut on his forehead that was bleeding freely, and Grandma Joyce was holding her wrist at an odd angle, but they were alive.

As Kaelyn made her way to them, stumbling over overturned chairs and debris, the full extent of the damage became clear. More than half of the beautiful Cherrywood bar was in splinters, its centuries-old craftsmanship reduced to rubble in seconds. Several people lay unmoving amid the debris, while others moaned in pain or called out for help.

"We need to get out of here," Grandpa Terry said, his voice hoarse from the smoke. He struggled to his feet, helping Grandma Joyce up with his free hand while the other pressed a napkin to his bleeding forehead.

"We should help the injured," her grandma urged, but she was cut off by a harsh cough.

"We need to get you out of here. Your arm doesn't look good. I'll come back and help once you and Kaelyn are safe."

Kaelyn nodded, coughing. "The front windows blew out. Maybe . . . maybe we should go out the side door? There may be less glass."

They made their way slowly through the devastated dining room toward the side door, helping others where they could, but not taking too much time. The smoke was getting thicker, making it harder to see and breathe. Kaelyn's eyes stung, and her lungs burned with each breath.

As they neared the staircase leading to the hotel rooms upstairs, a figure emerged from the smoke. It was the busboy who had been humming earlier. His uniform was torn and stained with soot, and there was a wild look in his eyes that prompted Kaelyn to take a step back.

"It's beautiful, isn't it?" he said, his voice dreamy and distant. "The fire, the destruction. It's what The One wants."

"Who?" Kaelyn found herself asking, even as her instincts screamed at her to run. "Who wants this?"

The busboy's face split into a wide, unsettling grin. "Can't you hear them singing? He numbers the stars. The One knows."

Before anyone could react, he launched into the now-familiar tune. "Twinkle, twinkle, little star . . ."

Grandpa Terry grabbed Kaelyn's good arm and pulled her away. "We need to go. Now."

The heat from the fire intensified. Staff and guests were in disarray. Some were injured, and everyone was confused and upset. As Kaelyn and her grandparents joined the exodus, she couldn't help but look back.

The busboy stood in the hallway near the Governor's Room and banquet hall, still singing as flames licked at the walls around him. His eyes met Kaelyn's for a moment, and she saw something there that would haunt her for days to come. A mixture of madness and ecstasy, as if he were experiencing something profoundly life changing in the midst of this horror.

Then they were outside, gulping in the fresh air as they stumbled away from the burning building. Sirens wailed in the distance, signaling the approach of emergency services. All around them, dazed survivors gathered in small groups, some crying, others staring blankly at the inferno that had once been the historic Irma Hotel.

A flood of questions rushed through Kaelyn's head as she huddled close to her grandparents. Two violent incidents in one day, in sleepy Cody of all places? And that song. First the shooter at the doctor's office, and now the busboy with the same childhood tune. It couldn't be a coincidence, could it?

As paramedics arrived and tended to the injured, Kaelyn caught snippets of conversation from those around her.

". . . just like the attacks in the big cities . . ."

". . . some kind of coordinated terror campaign?"

". . . something similar happened in Casper about an hour ago."

". . . what if it spreads? What if nowhere is safe anymore?"

The world she knew was changing rapidly, becoming more dangerous by the moment. And Kaelyn couldn't shake the feeling that this was only the beginning. Whatever was happening didn't seem to be only here.

She quietly resolved to find out what was going on. She suspected the two incidents were linked, and if so, she wanted to understand why.

Chapter 3

The pungent scent of smoke clung to the air around Kaelyn and her grandparents as they stood across the street from the Irma Hotel. The once-stately building now bore the scars of the explosion in its kitchen. Shattered windows and blackened walls marked its historic facade. Emergency vehicles crowded the streets, their lights flashing silently against the backdrop of the afternoon sun, casting an unsettling glow over the scene.

A young paramedic approached them, his face etched with concern as he gave a quick examination. "I'm sorry," he addressed Grandma Joyce, "but I'm afraid your wrist is broken. We'll need to get you to the hospital for proper treatment."

Grandma Joyce attempted a smile, though it came out more as a grimace. "Well, looks like Kaelyn and I will be twinsies now. Matching injuries and all."

The joke fell flat, the gravity of the situation too heavy for humor. Kaelyn managed a weak nod, her own arm throbbing where she'd fallen on it during the explosion.

The paramedic turned to Grandpa Terry. "Sir, given that this is a mass casualty event, our resources are stretched thin. Do you feel well enough to drive your wife to the hospital? Her injury isn't life-threatening, but she does need medical attention."

Grandpa Terry straightened, his voice firm despite the cut on his forehead. "Yes, I can manage that. But what about Kaelyn? She fell on her injured arm during the explosion. It needs to be checked too."

The paramedic nodded, glancing at her arm in its sling. "You're right. She should be examined as well. You can take her along to the hospital, but I must warn you, there might be a long wait given the circumstances."

"We understand," her grandpa said as he helped Grandma Joyce to her feet. "Thank you for your help."

"Terry?" Grandma Joyce said after the paramedic left. "There's Tylenol in my purse. Please get three each for Kaelyn and me?"

"You going to dry swallow them?" he asked as he dug them out.

She lifted her chin toward a soda machine under the covered porch of the Irma. "Think it's possible the pop machine is working? And you can somehow slip by and get us a drink?"

He chuckled. "Think they'll let me get close enough to use it?"

"Maybe?"

"I'll give it a go."

Kaelyn and her grandma watched as he made his way across the street and to the vending machine. No one seemed to even notice the old man in the cowboy boots who walked like he owned the place. Kaelyn felt like cheering when he bent over and retrieved the drink.

He glanced both ways before crossing back to them in a quick shuffle. "Here you go. Hope you don't mind sharing. I only had enough change for one. It had an option to use my credit card, but that seemed wrong."

After they each took the pain relievers, Grandma Joyce told Kaelyn she could have the rest of the soda. Sheridan Avenue, the main street through town and the direct route to the hospital, was blocked off. Grandpa Terry supported his wife as they walked to his truck. He had a habit of parking on Beck Avenue, the street behind the Irma Hotel.

Her grandma, however, had parked in the lot next to the hotel and restaurant. Currently, her car had another one sitting on top of it. Kaelyn hadn't seen it, but Grandpa Terry had checked on the car while her grandma was awaiting medical evaluation. He'd told them he saw it from the alley but didn't dare get any closer. The entire parking lot was a mess.

After helping both women into the vehicle, he fired up the big diesel. There were volunteers directing traffic, motioning him to take 12th Street to avoid the first responders. Alger Avenue was open, but staying on 12th, which turned into Cody Avenue, would be a more direct route. They'd end up on the back side of the high school, come out by the football field, and circle back to the hospital on Sheridan Avenue.

Traffic was heavy on the usually quiet street, with people being rerouted around the downtown area. Tourists, frustrated by the unexpected detour, honked their horns and shouted from their car windows. Tempers flared as drivers navigated the congested roads, adding to the confusion. The scene stood in sharp contrast to a typical peaceful day in Cody, with the usual calm atmosphere now filled with tension and impatience.

Kaelyn leaned back against her seat, the ache in her arm almost as bad as the ache in her heart. She should have done something when she heard him humming—as soon as she noticed it was the same song the guy at the doctor's office was humming.

But why? Why did they hum a kid's song? It didn't make any sense. Who cares if people hum? But the busboy was so weird—freaky—when they saw him. Spouting off about whatever craziness he was saying. Was he behind the explosion? If he was, did he make it out so the authorities could ask him why he did it?

As they approached the hospital, they could see the parking lot was full, with cars haphazardly parked on the grass and along the curbs. "We'll park at the museum," Grandpa Terry said, pulling into the Buffalo Bill Center of the West.

After finding a spot to park in the congested lot, he said, "You two, sit tight. I'll come around and open your doors and help you out. I know you're both feeling rather puny, and I don't want you to fall out of the truck."

Kaelyn couldn't help but smile. Her grandpa was a true gentleman. He made it sound like he was doing something out of the ordinary, but he always opened her grandma's door. Kaelyn's too. Her dad had the same manners.

She used to think it was old-fashioned, but now she appreciated the small gestures of kindness and respect. But she also understood not all women appreciated the gesture, and both her dad and granddad would sometimes get dirty looks when going out of their way to hold a door.

Inside, the emergency room was a scene of semi-controlled pandemonium. Medical staff rushed back and forth, their voices raised to be heard over the din of distressed patients. The waiting room was packed, nearly every chair occupied and people lining the walls.

They managed to find three seats together, wedged between a man with a nasty-looking gash on his arm and a woman comforting a child with a makeshift splint on her leg. A television mounted on the wall played the news, its volume barely audible over the noise in the room.

The man acknowledged them. "Were you at the hotel too?"

"In the restaurant," Grandpa Terry replied. "You?"

"My room. Upstairs. It could be worse. The room two doors down is gone. Just gone."

As the hours crawled by, Kaelyn found herself drawn to the images flashing across the screen. The ticker at the bottom scrolled continually, each new headline more alarming than the last.

"Multiple Cities Hit by Coordinated Bombings."

"Thousands Dead."

"Casualties Mount as Chaos Unfolds Across the Country."

"Breaking: Multiple Explosions Rock Casper, Wyoming."

Kaelyn's eyes widened at the mention of Casper. She racked her brain, trying to remember if she knew anyone there. It wasn't too far from Cody, only about four hours by car, but she couldn't recall any specific connections.

The thought of this violence spreading, reaching other parts of Wyoming and around the country, sent a chill down her spine. Even though there had been smaller events in the past weeks, today unfolded as a scene of death and destruction. Something big was happening, she had no doubt.

"Grandpa," she whispered, leaning closer to him, "do we know anyone in Casper?"

He furrowed his brow, thinking. "Well, sure. Remember my friends from church? The Kidwells? They moved there to be closer to their grandkids. Why do you ask?"

Kaelyn gestured toward the TV. "They're saying there were explosions there too. I wondered if we should be worried about anyone we know."

Her grandfather patted her hand gently. "I'm sure they're fine. But . . . can you tell where the explosions happened?"

"There were a lot of explosions. The first was by the mall, but I didn't recognize any of the other places. Sorry."

"I doubt they'd be at the mall." He waggled his eyebrows at her. "I'm sure they're fine, but we should be praying for all of those in danger." He paused a moment as he took in the screen. "It does look bad."

A man sitting nearby, his leg bouncing nervously as he waited for news of a loved one, spoke up. "Did you hear about that doctor? The one who thinks this craziness is caused by some kind of virus?"

Kaelyn and her grandparents turned toward him, their curiosity piqued.

"What do you mean, a virus?" Grandma Joyce asked, her voice laced with concern. "Like the pandemic?"

"Nah, not like that." He paused. "Well . . . maybe a little like that." The man leaned in and lowered his voice. "There was this doctor on the news earlier. He was saying all these incidents might be caused by some new kind of virus. Says we need to develop a new vaccine or something to stop it."

"A virus making people violent?" Kaelyn asked. "Is that even possible?"

The man shrugged. "I don't know. Sounds crazy, right? But after everything that's happened . . . who knows what's possible anymore."

Their conversation was interrupted by a nurse calling out, "Joyce Fisher?"

"Here!" Her grandpa raised his hand. "Can my granddaughter come back too? She needs to be seen."

The irritation in the nurse's demeanor was apparent. "She'll need to wait until it's her turn."

"Sure. That's fine." Grandpa Terry smiled at the woman. "But I'm not leaving her alone out here."

"Fine. Bring them both." She gave an exaggerated sigh. "I'll make a special effort to find her chart and give you priority treatment." She smirked.

As they reached the door being held open, Grandpa Terry said, "I appreciate your kindness, Miss. Things are a little too crazy today for me to feel comfortable being separated from my granddaughter or my wife. I'm sure you understand."

She softened her face and posture. "I do. Probably more than you can imagine. I'm sorry you were injured in the explosion. Please follow me."

"Not just that," Grandpa Terry said as they trailed behind her. "They were at the doctor's office when it had the trouble."

Kaelyn heard the nurse gasp. "You were at Dr. Newton's office?"

"We were," Grandma Joyce replied. "Kaelyn was having a follow-up for her surgery. She was seeing his associate. We haven't heard— "

"This way," she said, leading them into an exam room. When she turned to face them, tears were traveling down her face. "I knew Dr. Newton. He worked here."

"Knew?" Kaelyn said.

She gave a slow nod. "It's terrible."

"Do you know about the other deaths?" Kaelyn asked, her heart pounding hard.

"A receptionist and a nurse." She paused and her voice went hard. "A couple of patients. Plus, the shooter." She cleared her throat. "Let me go see if I can find your chart. What's your name?"

"Kaelyn Fisher." Her voice squeaked as she recalled the woman with her arm in a sling, her dress visible beneath the sheet as she lay dead on the ground.

"I'll be right back. I'll do both of your intakes at the same time."

"Those poor people," Grandma Joyce said. "I know I never met Dr. Newton, but your parents spoke highly of him. Said he had an excellent bedside manner."

Kaelyn nodded. "I guess. I was . . . I was kind of out of it. I don't even remember what he looked like." She closed her eyes to try and picture him but could only see the guy with the broken leg and the completely lost look on his face as he gazed off into the distance. The shooter.

The nurse returned. "Found it. Let's get you both ready to see the doc."

After she took their vitals and history, she said she hoped it wouldn't be long, but she wasn't sure. "I'm sure you all are exhausted after your day."

"Miss?" Grandpa Terry said. "My granddaughter and my wife are in quite a bit of pain. Any chance of getting them something for it?"

"Let me see what I can do. We'll probably need to wait until the doctor evaluates you, but I'll try."

After only fifteen minutes or so, there was a knock on the door. A tired-looking doctor greeted them, followed by their nurse from before. He quickly assessed Grandma Joyce's wrist.

"It's a simple break," he confirmed, gently manipulating the injured area. "We'll take x-rays to confirm, but I don't expect anything else. We'll put you in a cast. It should heal well with proper care."

"No surgery?"

"Probably won't be necessary." The doctor turned his attention to Kaelyn. "And you, young lady. Let's take a look at your arm."

Kaelyn winced as the doctor examined her arm. She was still in a cast, so there wasn't much he could do other than look. "We'll need to get some x-rays to be sure, but I'm concerned about potential swelling given your recent surgery and today's trauma." He turned to the nurse. "Let's get them something for the pain."

The nurse smiled and gave Kaelyn a wink. "Right away, Doctor."

Eventually, Grandma Joyce was taken for an x-ray and Kaelyn soon followed. The x-ray process was quick but uncomfortable, probably less so with the pain reliever than it would have been without. But it still required Kaelyn to hold her arm in positions that sent sharp pains through her shoulder and elbow. When she returned to the room, her grandma's cast was nearly finished.

It took only minutes for the doctor to return with the x-ray results. "Good news is the hardware from your surgery seems to be intact." He pointed to the metallic pins visible in the x-ray. "However, I am concerned there may be swelling. We're going to remove the cast and put you in a splint. I want you to come back tomorrow for another x-ray and possible recasting, depending on how the swelling progresses."

As the nurse removed Kaelyn's cast and replaced it with a splint, Grandma Joyce reached out with her newly pink-casted arm, patting Kaelyn's knee. "See? Twinsies, just like I said. We'll match again tomorrow when you get your new cast."

This time, Kaelyn managed a small smile. Despite everything, her grandmother's efforts to lighten the mood were starting to break through her distress.

By the time they left the hospital, night had fallen. The drive home was quiet, each lost in their own thoughts about the day's events. Kaelyn watched the darkening streets of Cody go by. The town she'd known all her life was now alien and threatening.

At her grandparents' home, she retreated to her room, the familiar space offering little comfort. She sat on her bed, replaying the day's events in her mind. The man with the gun at the doctor's office, smiling at her and seeming friendly—normal, even—before shooting up the place and murdering several people. The busboy at the Irma, humming shortly before the explosion.

A wave of guilt washed over her. If only she'd said something when she first noticed the gun. If only she'd mentioned the busboy's singing and made the connection between the two incidents. Maybe the explosion could have been prevented. Lives could have been saved.

But the doubt returned. Would anyone have believed her? Or would they have dismissed her concerns, maybe even thought she was losing her mind? After all, what did a tune have to do with explosions and violence?

Round and round her thoughts went, an endless loop of "what ifs" and "if onlys." Her arm throbbed, the pain intensifying as the medication from the hospital began to wear off. She glanced at the bottle of strong painkillers on her nightstand, prescribed after her surgery.

After a moment's hesitation, Kaelyn reached for the bottle. She knew she shouldn't take them unless absolutely necessary, but the physical pain coupled with her emotional turmoil was becoming unbearable. She swallowed one of the pills with a sip of water and lay back on her bed, willing sleep to come.

As the medication began to take effect, her thoughts became hazy. The events of the day blurred together. The doctor's office, the Irma, the hospital, the news programs . . . it was all swirling in her mind like a confusing, terrifying kaleidoscope. The last thing she remembered before drifting off was the haunting melody that seemed to connect it all. "Twinkle, twinkle, little star . . ."

Chapter 4

Kaelyn sat at her desk, the early morning darkness still blanketing the room. She cradled her broken right arm, held tight against her body by the sling, while she scribbled in a notepad with her left hand. The events of the previous day replayed in her mind, each detail sharpening the sense of urgency gnawing at her.

She needed to talk to her grandparents about what she'd noticed. But first, she wanted to get her thoughts in order.

Using her regular journal seemed wrong for this task, so Kaelyn opted for a steno notebook instead. The separate columns were perfect for listing pros and cons. She was aware she was complicating things, but without a clear outline of details, she would struggle to explain them to her grandparents.

Maybe calling her mom would help. Her mom had a knack for helping her only child express herself. Journaling and writing out her thoughts had been something her mom had started her on.

She checked the time on her phone. Almost five. In East Africa, where her parents were, it was eight hours ahead, making it one in the afternoon there. They were likely at the building site after resting at the hotel the night before.

She thought back to their planning sessions, back when she could still go, knowing the drive to the school they were working on was a lengthy one. They were probably deep into the day's work, at least halfway through, with the departing crew showing them the ropes.

With spotty cell service and reliable internet only being at their temporary housing, reaching her mom was impossible. Maybe in three or four hours, she'd have better luck. The workday should be over, and her parents would likely be back in their room.

Glancing out the window, she was happy to see the sky beginning to lighten. Her grandparents would be up soon, if they weren't already. Her grandpa liked to say the sun was his alarm clock. Usually, Kaelyn would still be sleeping. She was only up now because her arm had started throbbing. She took an over-the-counter pain reliever, but she hadn't been able to get comfortable again.

Tilting her head, she listened for movement in the house. A small smile spread across her face. It sounded like they were in the kitchen. Her grandpa was probably starting the coffee while her grandma asked him what he wanted for breakfast.

Kaelyn pushed herself up from her chair, wincing as pain shot through her arm. The splint was awkward and tight, a reminder of yesterday's trouble. She took a deep breath, steeling herself for the conversation ahead, and caught a whiff of bacon. Yep, they were up. She smiled to herself. Surely, Grandma Joyce had heard the humming too. Once Kaelyn mentioned it, her grandmother would probably make the connection as well.

Grabbing her notebook, she made her way to the kitchen, where the aroma of coffee mingled with the scent of bacon. To her surprise, she found Grandpa Terry at the stove, spatula in hand and grandma's apron tied around his waist.

"Morning, sunshine," he greeted her with a warm smile. "How's your arm feeling?"

"Sore," Kaelyn admitted, sinking into a chair at the kitchen table. "Where's Grandma?"

His expression softened. "She's still resting. Had a rough night with that broken wrist of hers. Figured I'd let her sleep in a bit."

He turned back to the stove, flipping the bacon without any difficulty. "Oh, by the way, we heard from your parents last night."

Kaelyn perked up at that. "You did? How?"

"Your grandma had me send one of those emails from her phone." He chuckled, shaking his head. "Surprised they could read it with as many letters as I missed. My fingers are too fat for that business."

He plated the bacon and set it on the table before pouring Kaelyn a glass of orange juice. "Anyway, they said they could come home. With what happened and your grandma's wrist broken . . ." He paused, studying Kaelyn's face. "Your grandma and I think things will be fine. It's not like you're hard to look after. I think this old man can handle it. But if you want them home . . ."

Kaelyn was conflicted. Part of her desperately wanted her parents back, craving the comfort and security their presence would bring. But she also knew how much this trip meant to them. They'd been planning and saving for over a year, working things out with their businesses to take the time off. People were counting on them.

"I'm fine, Grandpa," she said finally, mustering a smile. "They should stay. It's important work they're doing."

He nodded, a hint of pride in his eyes. "That's my girl. Now, let's get some food in you before we head back to the hospital."

As they ate breakfast, Kaelyn debated bringing up what she'd noticed about the humming. But without Grandma

Joyce there to corroborate her memories, she decided to hold off. She needed to make sure she remembered things the same way.

"What do you have there? Poetry? One of your stories?"

Kaelyn slid the notebook closer to herself. "N-no. Nothing like that."

"I do like your stories. You have such a flair for the dramatic. A real imagination. I think you should start entering them into some of those writing contests your mom mentioned."

"Maybe, but . . ." She shook her head. "You all think I'm an okay writer— "

"You're a great writer."

She shrugged. "I don't think I want a bunch of people reading my stuff."

"I know it's hard to put yourself out there, but you've got a real gift. Your stories are so imaginative."

"Thanks, Grandpa," she muttered. *A flair for the dramatic,* she thought. *Is that what he'll think when I tell them about the connection between the two men and their unsettling humming?*

When it was time to leave for the hospital, Grandma Joyce opted to stay home, the pain and discomfort from her broken wrist making her reluctant to venture out. Grandpa Terry helped Kaelyn into the truck, and they set off toward the hospital.

The emergency room was still busy, but not as crazy as the day before. They were directed to a different area for her follow-up, where a nurse quickly took her vitals before ushering them into an exam room.

An unfamiliar doctor entered. "I see you were here yesterday," he said, reviewing Kaelyn's chart. "I've reviewed the notes. Let's take another look at your arm, shall we?"

After a brief examination, the doctor ordered another set of x-rays. Kaelyn endured the uncomfortable process once again, gritting her teeth as her arm was manipulated into various positions.

When he returned with the results, his brow was furrowed in concentration. "I'd like to have someone else take a look at these," he said. "Someone from Dr. Newton's practice. For now, I think it's best to leave your arm in the splint. Keep from moving your arm too much and keep it in the sling."

Kaelyn nodded, a mixture of relief and frustration washing over her. She was glad nothing seemed seriously wrong, but the lack of a definitive answer was annoying.

"Until other arrangements are made, the remaining doctors from Newton's practice will be working out of the hospital," the doctor continued. "Stop at the front desk on your way out, and they'll make an appointment for you to come back before the end of the week. I'm sorry for all the back and forth, but things are disorganized right now, as you can well imagine."

As they left the hospital, Grandpa Terry suggested they take Sheridan Avenue on the way home. They had taken a roundabout route to the hospital, unsure if the road was open, but he had learned while they were there that it had reopened overnight. "Might as well see how things are looking downtown," he said, his voice heavy with concern.

As they drove down Sheridan, the destruction of the Irma Hotel and Restaurant came into view. Kaelyn's chest tightened, her breathing becoming shallow and rapid. The historic building, once a proud landmark of Cody, now stood partially collapsed, its windows shattered and walls blackened by smoke.

"You okay, sweetheart?" Grandpa Terry asked, glancing at her with worry.

She nodded, not trusting her voice. What was wrong with her? Why was she reacting so strongly?

They turned by the Walgreens, heading down Big Horn Avenue toward her grandparents' house on the outskirts of Cody. The familiar streets helped calm Kaelyn's nerves, the rhythm of the drive lulling her into a sense of normalcy.

"Do you need to stop by your house?" he asked, slowing as he neared the street that would lead them to the home she shared with her parents. "Need anything from there?"

"No, I think I'm fine. We watered the houseplants yesterday morning. Grandma checked, and the sprinklers were still set on the timer for the outdoor stuff. We don't need to go by until tomorrow or the next day."

He sped back up. As they left the business area and rounded a bend, a car appeared in their lane, heading straight for them. Kaelyn's heart leaped into her throat as she realized the vehicle wasn't slowing down or moving over.

"Grandpa!" she cried out in warning.

Grandpa Terry's reflexes, honed by years of Wyoming driving, kicked in. He swerved hard to the right, the truck's tires squealing in protest. For a terrifying moment, Kaelyn thought they might flip, but her grandfather managed to keep control.

The oncoming car, however, wasn't so lucky. As it sped past them, the driver seemed to realize their mistake too late. They overcorrected, sending the vehicle into a spin.

With a sickening crunch of metal on metal, the car slammed into a parked truck before flipping onto its roof.

Grandpa Terry brought the truck to a screeching halt. "Stay here," he ordered, his voice tight with tension as he jumped out.

Kaelyn watched, her heart pounding, as her grandfather rushed toward the overturned car. Other drivers had stopped as well, and a small crowd gathered around the wreckage. She could hear shouts for someone to call 9-1-1 and could see people trying to peer into the crushed vehicle.

The wait seemed endless, as Kaelyn tried to catch glimpses of what was happening. The truck was parked against the curb and several vehicles, including a firetruck and ambulance, were between her and the wrecked car. At last, Grandpa Terry returned to the truck, his face pale and drawn.

"Is . . . is the driver okay?" she asked, already dreading the answer.

He shook his head slowly. "No, sweetheart. She didn't make it."

The drive home was conducted in heavy silence, the weight of what they'd witnessed pressing down on them both. Kaelyn stared out the window, her mind replaying the accident over and over. How quickly things had changed, how fragile life now seemed.

As they pulled into their driveway, Grandpa Terry turned off the engine but made no move to get out. He sat there for a moment, his hands still gripping the steering wheel.

"Kaelyn," he said finally, his voice rough with emotion, "I want you to know how proud I am of you. You've been so brave through all of this."

Tears pricked at her eyes. "I don't feel brave," she admitted.

"Being brave doesn't mean you're not scared. It means you keep going even when you are scared. And that's exactly what you've been doing."

He reached out and squeezed her good hand. "We're going to get through this, you hear me? Whatever's happening in Cody, whatever's going on in the world, we're going to be okay."

Kaelyn nodded, a lump forming in her throat. As they got out of the truck and headed toward the house, she couldn't shake the feeling their lives had changed irrevocably. The Cody she knew, the safe haven of her childhood, seemed to be slipping away with each passing hour.

But her grandfather's words echoed in her mind. They were going to be okay. She wanted to believe that. She had to believe it.

Chapter 5

As Kaelyn and her grandfather entered the house, they found Grandma Joyce dozing in her recliner. The soft click of the door roused her, and she blinked awake, her eyes quickly focusing on their somber expressions.

"What's wrong?" she asked, sitting up straighter and wincing as she jostled her broken wrist.

Grandpa Terry sighed heavily, sinking into his armchair. "There was a car accident on our way home."

"An accident?" Grandma Joyce's eyes widened. "Are you both all right?"

"We're fine," Kaelyn assured her, perching on the arm of the sofa. "Grandpa missed colliding with her. But the other driver . . . she didn't make it."

Grandma Joyce shook her head, her face etched with concern. "So many things happening. I was watching the news earlier, but I had to turn it off. It's all too much."

She paused, looking between Kaelyn and Grandpa Terry. "Some Wyoming counties are under a state of emergency. They didn't mention Park County. I guess the Irma damage wasn't enough. Five people dead wasn't enough." She shook her head again. "Of course, a car accident, that's just an accident, right?"

Grandpa Terry shrugged as his brow furrowed. "Why wouldn't it be?"

"I don't know. There's so much happening. The world has gone crazy. Thank the Lord you're both okay."

"The woman was still alive when I reached her. She was . . . out of her head, singing some old song I couldn't quite recognize."

Kaelyn froze, her heart racing. "Was it 'Twinkle, Twinkle, Little Star'?" she asked, her voice barely above a whisper.

"No, no." Her grandpa shook his head. "It was a pop song. Some singer from the '80s who went by one name. The woman is still around, though I'll say, she looks a might different than she used to. That cow poison didn't do her any favors."

"What cow poison?" her grandma asked.

"What song?" Kaelyn pressed, leaning forward.

He lifted his hands in a gesture of uncertainty. "Don't remember the name of it. Some pop song she kept repeating one line of. Off-tune and gasping for breath. It was the freakiest thing."

"What was the song about?" Grandma Joyce asked.

"Something about a star shining."

"A star?"

"Yup. A lucky star."

"She was singing about a star?" Kaelyn asked, her mind reeling. Could it be? The other two men were humming about stars, but in a kids' song instead of some song from the olden days. "The car aimed straight for us."

"I guess," her grandpa said before turning to his wife. "Can I get you anything? I bet you're hungry. Let me make us an early lunch."

As he busied himself in the kitchen, Kaelyn's thoughts raced. Three incidents, three people singing about stars before committing violent acts. It couldn't be a coincidence, could it?

Throughout the day, they watched the news off and on while Kaelyn also scanned her phone. The reports were grim. The troubles were getting worse, spreading to more cities, more countries. She tried calling her parents several times but couldn't get through. The news anchors speculated the phone networks were being affected, possibly due to overuse as people frantically tried to reach loved ones.

Kaelyn searched for news about East Africa, relief washing over her when she found no reports of similar incidents there. At least her parents were probably safe.

As evening approached and they sat down to dinner, Kaelyn decided it was time to share her suspicions. She took a deep breath, steeling herself.

"Grandma, Grandpa, I need to tell you something," she began, her voice wavering slightly. "I think . . . I think there's a connection between all these incidents. The ones here in Cody, at least."

Her grandparents exchanged a glance before turning their attention back to her. "What do you mean, sweetie?" Grandma Joyce asked gently.

Kaelyn laid it all out. The man at the doctor's office humming, the busboy singing, and now the woman in the car accident. All singing about stars before violent acts.

As she spoke, she saw her grandparents' expressions shift from curiosity to concern. When she finished, silence hung heavy in the air.

Finally, Grandpa Terry spoke. "That sounds like a good basis for a story, Kaelyn, but don't you think it's a little too close to real life?"

"It's not a story," she insisted, her voice rising. "This is what happened. Grandma, you heard the man in the doctor's office, right? You heard him humming?"

Grandma Joyce hesitated. "Well . . . maybe. I wasn't paying much attention."

"What about the busboy?" Kaelyn pressed. "He went by us humming the song. Right before he blew up the Irma."

"We don't know the busboy was responsible," Grandpa Terry said gently. "The news is saying it was a gas leak and isn't related to the events in other places. It was an accident."

"Do you believe that's the truth?" Kaelyn asked, her confidence beginning to waver.

Her grandparents shared another look before Grandma Joyce spoke. "I'd hate to think some young man would want to blow up the Irma and kill all those people."

"The shooter in the doctor's office couldn't have been much older than me," Kaelyn countered. "And the lady driving the car, she aimed straight for us. Grandpa said she was singing too. Who sings when they're injured and dying?"

"But you said the boys were humming before they committed their atrocities," Grandpa Terry pointed out. "The woman was singing when I found her. After she'd already crashed. And we don't know if she was aiming for us. She may have lost control or . . . or . . ."

"Or had a medical emergency," Grandma Joyce added. "How old was she?"

"Not old. Maybe early thirties."

Her grandparents smiled at her sweetly, but their eyes held a mixture of concern and doubt. "It's unlikely the incidents are related, sweetie," Grandma Joyce said softly. "I know you have a wonderful imagination, but sometimes things are simply coincidences."

Kaelyn's shoulders sagged. They didn't believe her. She'd laid out all the evidence, pointed out the connections, and they still thought she was making up stories.

"But . . ." she started, before trailing off. What else could she say? How could she make them understand?

"It's okay, Kaelyn." Grandpa Terry reached for her hand. "These are scary times, and it's natural to try to find patterns to make sense of things. But sometimes, bad things happen, and there's no big conspiracy behind them."

She nodded, not trusting herself to speak. She'd been so sure, so certain she'd figured something out. But now, faced with her grandparents' gentle skepticism, she felt foolish. Maybe they were right. Maybe it was her overactive imagination, seeing connections where there were none.

As they finished dinner, the conversation turned to other topics—how Grandma Joyce's wrist was feeling, whether they needed to go grocery shopping soon, and if they should check on the neighbors. Kaelyn participated half-heartedly, her mind still churning over her theory.

Later that night, as she lay in bed, Kaelyn stared at the ceiling, replaying the conversation in her head. She'd been so confident when she'd written everything down in her notebook, but when it came time to share her thoughts, she'd faltered. Her grandparents' doubt had shaken her, making her question everything she thought she knew.

Was she imagining things? Making connections that weren't there? She'd always had a vivid imagination. It's what made her a good writer, after all. But this was different. This was real life, with real consequences.

Kaelyn rolled onto her side, wincing as she jostled her injured arm. She wanted so badly to believe she was right, that she'd stumbled onto something important. But the more she thought about it, the more ridiculous it seemed.

People singing about stars causing violence? It sounded like the plot of a bad science fiction movie.

She thought about calling her mom again, wondering if she'd have better luck getting through. It was early morning there. She'd be up, getting ready to go work. Her mom always listened to her ideas, no matter how far-fetched they might seem.

But even as she reached for her phone, she hesitated. What if her mom reacted the same way as her grandparents? What if she, too, thought Kaelyn was letting her imagination run wild?

With a sigh, she set her phone back on the nightstand. Maybe it was better to wait, to see if she could find more evidence before sharing her theory again. She didn't want to worry her parents unnecessarily, especially when they were so far away and couldn't do anything to help.

She picked the phone up again. She wouldn't call her mom, but she wasn't tired. She nestled it against a pillow and started scrolling. The same old same old. Trouble around the world. She did a search to make sure her parents were still safe in Africa. There was a report of an incident, but it was in a city far from where her parents were building the school.

On a whim, she typed in "Twinkle, Twinkle, Little Star." She got the usual nursery rhyme info and links to watch videos of the song. She was about to set her phone aside when her eye caught a conversation on the popular EchoChamber website.

The preview featured someone recounting how they had heard humming seconds before a woman shoved a man in front of a bus. "It was the nursery rhyme, 'Twinkle, Twinkle, Little Star.'"

Kaelyn clicked on the link. There were dozens of posts in the thread. Some mentioned they heard singing, too, before the singer suddenly turned violent, but it wasn't the nursery rhyme. One said it was a song by Madonna, while another claimed it was a Bob Dylan tune and someone else said it was a popular Ed Sheeran song.

Then one post gave her a chill. "Dudes, they're calling them Star Brights. They go into like a trance, start humming or singing songs with the word star in the lyrics or title, and pretty soon they're killers. The government knows about this, but they aren't doing anything to stop it. Not only aren't they stopping it, they're in on it."

Kaelyn's heart raced as she read through the EchoChamber posts. The term "Star Brights" jumped out at her, confirming her suspicions and sending a chill down her spine. She wasn't alone in noticing the connection between the singing and the violent incidents. It wasn't her imagination.

It was real.

She searched for more information using the term "Star Bright." Post after post described similar experiences. People humming or singing songs about stars before committing acts of violence. Some accounts mentioned "Twinkle, Twinkle, Little Star," while others referenced pop songs, obscure folk tunes, and even "The Star-Spangled Banner." The common thread was always the same: stars in the lyrics, followed by inexplicable violence.

As she delved deeper into the online discussions, Kaelyn experienced a mixture of vindication and growing unease. Her theory wasn't the product of an overactive imagination. Others had noticed the same pattern. But the implications were terrifying. If this was happening all over, on a scale large enough for people around the world to notice, why wasn't it being addressed officially?

One post caught her attention. "My brother's girlfriend's uncle works for the CDC. He says they're working on something to combat it and an announcement should be made soon. But I think there's more going on than he's saying. Much more, and they're keeping us in the dark."

Kaelyn's mind whirled with possibilities. Was this a government cover-up? Or was it simply another conspiracy theory with people on the internet connecting dots that weren't actually there? She thought back to her grandparents' skepticism and their gentle dismissal of her concerns.

As the night wore on, she continued to read, alternating between feeling validated and questioning her own sanity. The more she learned, the more questions she had. Why stars? What was triggering this behavior? And most importantly, how could it be stopped?

Around midnight, her eyes heavy with fatigue, Kaelyn finally set her phone aside. Her mind was a jumble of information, theories, and fears. Part of her wanted to wake her grandparents, to show them what she'd found and prove she wasn't imagining things. But another part hesitated, remembering their earlier reactions.

With her arm aching, she reached for the pain pill on the nightstand, not the heavy-duty ones but the regular strength. Kaelyn had made a decision. She would keep investigating, gathering as much information as she could.

But she'd be smart about it. No more blurting out theories without solid evidence, and not only from EchoChamber posts. She knew her grandparents didn't take much stock in most of the social media platforms, assuming they were pretty much the equivalent of gossip magazines.

No, she'd find other sources. News articles and information they would pay attention to. She'd document everything and build a case even her skeptical grandparents couldn't dismiss.

Chapter 6

Kaelyn sat in the shade of an umbrella, watching her grandfather work in the garden. The midmorning sun was already intense, its heat shimmering off the rows of vegetables. Grandpa Terry moved between the plants with practiced ease, his weathered hands gently tending to each one.

"Are you sure we can't help?" Grandma Joyce called from her seat next to Kaelyn. Her broken wrist rested in her lap, the cast a brilliant pink that coordinated nicely with her floral sundress. The pattern reminded Kaelyn of the dress worn by the woman at the doctor's office, one of the victims of the humming guy.

Her grandpa straightened, wiping sweat from his brow. "You two focus on healing. I've got this under control. If this heat keeps up, the garden'll be bursting before we know it."

"What we need is a good, soaking rain."

"Wouldn't surprise me if we get one. Storm clouds are stacking up in the west."

Kaelyn glanced over her shoulder at the darkening sky.

"Don't let him fool you," her grandma said. "He's no cloud-reader. He checked the weather this morning."

"I heard that!" Grandpa Terry shook a finger in their direction. "A smart farmer uses the information he has available. No shame in that."

"If you say so, dear."

Kaelyn shifted in her chair, feeling restless as she listened to her grandparents' banter. Her arm ached dully in its sling. She should be in Africa with her parents, but no. Her clumsiness had brought her to this point, where everything was in upheaval. It wasn't the first time she'd tripped over her own feet, but these were definitely the worst results.

At least she was with her grandparents. Her grandpa was doing all he could to take care of them, but she knew it was taking a toll on him, and it had only been two days since the explosion at the Irma. She gazed out over the property, taking in the familiar sights.

Sitting in the garden at the back of her grandparents' yard, Kaelyn took in the view of the lovingly tended acre of land that stretched out before her. The vegetable garden covered a good stretch of land, its neat rows promising tomatoes, peppers, and squash.

For now, they were just green shoots pushing through the soil. The growing season in Wyoming was just underway. They'd planted a few of the heartier vegetables over Mother's Day weekend, as they did every year. Her family had joined them and followed with supper. Sometimes the planting was done between spurts of snow. Snow on Mother's Day was common.

The rest of the garden waited until after Memorial Day, when her grandparents worked on planting a few rows each day until they were done. Each year, they said they were going to put in a smaller garden the next, but it always remained the same size or was even enlarged slightly.

Grandpa Terry said it kept them busy. They'd both been retired for over ten years from state jobs. They lived simply, which helped make their pensions go further. Their modest home was paid off and, thanks to the current market, worth more than they'd ever dreamed. But as her grandpa liked to say, "We can't afford to buy a new place, so we might as well stay where we are."

A patch of lawn separated the garden from the house, its grass a lush green despite the summer heat. At the far end of the property, a few dwarf fruit trees stood sentinel, their branches adorned with blossoms hinting at the apples and pears to come.

The neighboring houses stood clearly in view, each on a spacious lot, separated by wire-lined post-and-rail fences. It was a far cry from the cramped subdivisions in some towns, even much larger than the lot she and her parents lived on, offering a sense of privacy and connection to nature Kaelyn had always loved.

Her grandma had declared today to be a screen-free day until afternoon. No television. No computer. Not even scrolling on the phone, unless there was a valid reason. So far, they hadn't been able to reach her parents. They'd all tried calling and had sent emails, but there had yet to be a response. Was their nonresponse related to the troubles in the world?

Kaelyn's mind wandered back to her late-night research. The term "Star Brights" echoed in her thoughts, along with the countless stories she'd read of people experiencing the same phenomenon she'd noticed. A sense of validation washed over her, knowing she wasn't alone in her observations. But still, she hesitated to bring it up again. The memory of her grandparents' gentle dismissal stung, and she feared they still wouldn't believe her, even with this new information.

She was mentally cataloging the evidence, trying to figure out the best way to present it, when a scream shattered the quiet. Kaelyn jumped to her feet, her heel catching on the edge of her chair. The motion sent her stumbling forward, arms pinwheeling, before she caught herself with an awkward step.

"What was that?" Grandma Joyce gasped, already out of her chair and steady on her feet.

Grandpa Terry didn't wait for an answer; he headed toward the sound with long, steady strides. Kaelyn and her grandmother hurried after him, their injuries forgotten as they reached the fence line.

On the other side, Chloe Beckwith was sprawled near her clothesline, her overturned laundry basket spilling sheets across the grass.

"Chloe!" Grandpa Terry called, vaulting over the fence.

Kaelyn and Grandma Joyce slipped through the gate, reaching Chloe as Grandpa Terry helped her sit up.

"Oh, I'm so embarrassed," Chloe murmured, dabbing at her flushed face. "I got dizzy all of a sudden. Must be the heat."

Standing back slightly, Kaelyn surveyed the situation. She strained her ears, trying to catch any hint of the woman humming. The only sounds she could discern were the birds and other natural noises.

"Let's get you inside," Grandma Joyce said, her nurturing instincts kicking in despite her broken wrist. "Terry? Can you help her up?"

He helped Chloe to her feet and guided her into her house. Once inside, they settled her on the couch and Kaelyn fetched a glass of water while Grandpa Terry turned on the air conditioning.

"I'm fine, really," she protested weakly. "Just a silly spell. I shouldn't have worried you all."

"Nonsense," Grandma Joyce said firmly. "That's what neighbors are for. Now, have you eaten today? Have you been ill?"

"Well . . . not ill. I'm— " She flushed slightly. "We're going to have a baby. I think it was probably that. I've been feeling a little sick, and . . ." Chloe lifted her hands while her shoulders went to her ears.

"How wonderful!" Grandma Joyce clapped her hands together. "Congratulations."

"Yes, thank you. I wish I felt a little better."

As her grandmother fussed over Chloe, Kaelyn found herself scanning the room, half-expecting to see signs of something more sinister than a simple fainting spell. But everything looked normal. No evidence of violence, no humming, no singing. This wasn't a Star Bright incident.

After ensuring Chloe was comfortable and offering to check on her later, to which she replied there was no need, that she'd be fine and her husband would be home soon, they made their way back home. The excitement had worn Kaelyn out, her arm throbbing from the unexpected exertion.

"Why don't you rest for a bit?" Grandma Joyce suggested as they entered the house. "I think we could all use a break after that excitement."

Kaelyn nodded and retreated to her room. But instead of lying down, she pulled out her notebook. She began jotting down her thoughts about the Star Brights, organizing the information she'd gathered online. This time, she wouldn't back down. She'd present her case clearly and confidently, overcoming her usual timidity.

She was in the middle of rehearsing her argument when a knock at the door interrupted her thoughts.

"Kaelyn?" It was Grandpa Terry. "Can you come out to the living room?"

Curious and a bit apprehensive, she followed her grandfather. In the living room, she found both her grandparents seated on the couch, their expressions serious. The television was playing but the sound was off.

"Sit down, sweetie," Grandma Joyce said, motioning to the armchair across from them. "We owe you an apology."

Kaelyn's eyebrows shot up in surprise as she took a seat. "An apology? For what?"

Grandpa Terry leaned forward, his elbows resting on his knees. "We thought you were seeing patterns that weren't there, but it seems . . . well, we watched an interview on Wolf News. The announcer made it seem like the man he was interviewing was nuts, but . . . well, he said what you said."

"He said what I said?"

"Yes, about the troubles."

Kaelyn's heart began to race. "About the humming and singing?"

Grandma Joyce nodded. "People are singing or humming songs about stars, then they do . . . whatever they're going to do. Sometimes, they seem like they're in a trance before they come out of it for a minute. And they even sing afterward, if they survive what they did."

"Remember the earlier incident on the subway?" Grandpa Terry added. "The young girl who said she didn't do it, didn't use a kitchen knife to cut and stab people, but they had video of her doing it? She was dazed and confused and, apparently, singing through the entire thing. Anyway, the man said they call them Star Brights. Officially, it's all a rumor, but . . ." He raised his hands as he shook his head.

"I knew it!" Kaelyn exclaimed, unable to contain herself. "That's exactly what I found online. There are so many people talking about it, sharing their experiences. Why didn't you believe me when I told you?"

Her grandparents exchanged a guilty look. "We're sorry, Kaelyn," Grandma Joyce said softly. "We should have listened to you more carefully. It's . . . well, it all seemed so fantastical."

"But you believed it when you saw it on TV," she said, unable to keep the hurt from her voice.

Grandpa Terry sighed. "You're right. We should have trusted your judgment more. You're a smart girl, Kaelyn. We know that. I guess sometimes it's hard for us old folks to accept the world can change so dramatically, so quickly . . . without reason. Truth is, it doesn't make any sense."

A mix of emotions swirled inside her: vindication and relief, but also a lingering frustration. Why had it taken an outside source for them to believe her? Why couldn't they have trusted her in the first place?

"So, what do we do now?" she asked, pushing aside her conflicted feelings for the moment. "If this is truly happening, if the Star Brights are real, what does it mean for us?"

"Apparently, being disconnected this morning, while wonderful, meant we missed a few things. The CDC issued a warning about people acting strangely and urged calls to a special hotline or 9-1-1. The president spoke afterward. He's locking everything down again, closing federal buildings, post offices, and national parks."

"Yellowstone?"

"Yup. They're even limiting travel coming into the US. It's good your folks still have several weeks before they're coming home."

"Will they have trouble getting home?"

"Not by then, dear. Everything will be sorted out and fine." Even though her grandma said the words, Kaelyn didn't think she sounded convinced.

"Things are probably going to change for a while and be like they were during the pandemic. Seems California is even locking its borders. They've had quite a few incidents, so it might be for our safety as much as theirs." Her grandpa gave a low chuckle. "No one in or out of the state. Rumor is Oregon and Washington will be doing the same thing, probably some East Coast states too."

"So, we're going on lockdown?" Kaelyn's pulse rate accelerated. "What about school?"

"It's only the seventh of June. I'm sure things will be fine before school starts. Your senior year will be everything you hope for."

"Okay. If you say so." She leaned back in the chair.

Her grandma gestured in her direction. "You said you did some research? Do you want to share it with us?"

Kaelyn tilted her head. "Will it make a difference?"

Her grandparents shared a look she couldn't quite decipher. "We don't know, honey," she admitted. "But we'll figure it out together. And this time, we promise to listen to you. You've got good instincts, and we should have recognized that sooner."

Kaelyn nodded, feeling a warmth spread through her chest at her grandmother's words. It wasn't a complete resolution to her frustration, but it was a start. They believed her now, and that was what mattered most. Even if the world was falling apart around them.

"I have done research and taken notes," she said, sitting up straighter. "About the patterns I've noticed, the stories I've read online. Maybe, if we go through it all together, we can understand what's happening."

Her grandparents nodded. "I guess that wouldn't hurt," her grandma said.

"Do you think you two could get started without me?" Grandpa Terry asked. "I thought I'd make a run to the grocery store and the feed store."

"The feed store?" Kaelyn asked. "For what?"

Her grandma smiled. "They have more than livestock feed there."

Grandpa Terry put on his ballcap and went out the door, promising to be back soon.

"Well, dear, let's see your research," her grandma said with a smile, though the concern was still showing on her face.

As Kaelyn went to fetch her notebook, a new sense of purpose washed over her. They were finally taking her seriously, treating her like an adult with valuable insights to offer.

But as she returned to the living room, notebook in hand, a small part of her couldn't help but wonder, would they have believed her if it hadn't been for the TV interview? And what did it say about her relationship with her grandparents if it took an outside source to validate her observations?

Pushing these thoughts aside, Kaelyn opened her notebook and began to share her findings. Whatever doubts she had, whatever hurt lingered, could be dealt with later. Right now, they had a mystery to solve, and for the first time, they were truly in it together.

As she showed her notes, she experienced a growing sense of unity with her grandma. She listened attentively as Kaelyn outlined her theories, asked thoughtful questions, and even contributed her own observations. It was a far cry from her dismissive attitude of yesterday.

"Your grandpa's going to be so impressed by this," she said with a genuine smile. "This is amazing information. Incredibly detailed and thorough."

Kaelyn smiled as she leaned back in her chair.

Chapter 7

Kaelyn stared out the window, watching the rain cascade down in sheets. It had been overcast and drizzly for three days straight, but at least the intense heat from last week had eased. The gloomy weather seemed fitting, mirroring the mood that had settled over the town.

She tapped her cast, which had been replaced before things became too crazy and the hospital stopped taking all but emergency cases. Even with only emergencies, they'd heard the hospital was stretched thin and tents had been set up outside for triaging the patients, armed guards protecting the staff.

Today was Tuesday, June 13th, exactly one week since Cody, Wyoming, and the rest of the world had been upended. In just days, the town had shifted from a bustling tourist destination at the height of its season to a place weighed down by fear and uncertainty. The governor had declared martial law, though its effects in Cody were less severe than in Wyoming's larger cities.

Cheyenne and Casper, each home to around sixty thousand people, had been sealed off. No one was allowed in or out without official papers. Several other large towns were either locked down or on their way to it. Cody, for now, faced only minor travel restrictions, and no one seemed eager to enforce them. The governor had ordered people to stay put, but Kaelyn knew some were still slipping off to Powell or Meeteetse. Not her or her grandparents, but they'd heard of others.

That wouldn't last. Rumors pointed to roadblocks and National Guard escorts through town. Kaelyn knew strict border control was already in place on the East and West Coasts, as well as in neighboring Colorado, but she still couldn't believe it was happening in her hometown.

Her mind wandered back over the events of the past week. The first major Star Bright incident, after the Irma Hotel explosion, occurred while she was having her cast replaced, before the town fully shut down.

A tour bus driver, halfway through his spiel about Buffalo Bill Cody, had burst into song. According to survivors, "The Star-Spangled Banner" had never sounded so sinister. Before anyone could react, he'd driven the bus off the road and into the Shoshone River. The swift current had nearly swept the vehicle away before emergency services could arrive. Several fatalities had sent shockwaves through the community.

That same day, there was an incident at the Buffalo Bill Center of the West, a large well-known museum in Cody. Witnesses reported a museum docent began singing "Twinkle, Twinkle, Little Star" before attempting to destroy several priceless artifacts. The situation was contained, and there was no loss of life. They'd been in the process of closing the museum when the incident happened.

Losing the Irma Hotel, followed by the destruction at the museum, had people talking. The museum was one of Cody's most treasured institutions, a cornerstone of the community, and one of their claims of fame. People came from all over the world to view the collection of guns in the recently renovated Cody Firearms Museum, one of the five museums at the Center.

Tourists were already leaving due to the closure of Yellowstone and the onset of the lockdown. Initially, Wyoming's governor had not implemented a full lockdown, opting instead to follow the basic CDC recommendations. But only a short time later, as the violence spread, he changed his mind and instituted more stringent rules.

The governor urged everyone to stay home, following the example of leaders in other states. Restaurants and grocery stores were closed. Gas stations were operating on a limited basis. Basic food distributions were set up at various spots around town. They picked up their food in a parking lot on Big Horn Avenue.

"Kaelyn?" Her grandmother's voice broke through her reverie. "Can you help me with lunch?"

"Sure, Grandma," Kaelyn replied, tearing herself away from the window. As she entered the kitchen, she noticed her grandmother struggling with a manual can opener, her broken wrist still hampering her movements.

"Here, let me help," Kaelyn offered. Working together with Grandma Joyce holding the can and Kaelyn operating the mechanism, they were able to get the job done. "How's your wrist feeling?"

Grandma Joyce sighed. "Better, I suppose. Though I'll be glad when this cast comes off. Your arm?"

Kaelyn flexed her fingers, wincing slightly. "Not as much pain. Do you think the hospital will be open when my appointment time comes up?" When they'd replaced the cast, they made a follow-up appointment for four weeks. The plan was to do another x-ray to ensure the bones were healing properly. If they were, they'd discuss the next step.

"I'm hopeful," her grandma said with a smile. "Hopeful they'll be open when my cast is ready to come off too." Like Kaelyn, her grandma had an appointment scheduled.

To help with the logistics of it, they were on the same day at back-to-back times.

As they prepared a simple lunch of soup and sandwiches, Kaelyn's thoughts drifted back to the changes in Cody. The panic had set in quickly after the bus incident. Long-term residents, who had initially viewed the Star Bright phenomenon as something happening "elsewhere," were now looking at each other with skepticism. Even though most of the tourists had left, some remained. Those who lived a distance away weren't sure they'd be able to find fuel on the way home.

With gas stations in Cody operating on a limited basis, even locals were concerned about it. They were allowed two gallons per week, depending on the last digit of their license plate number.

Since her grandpa's plate ended with a five, his day was Tuesday. He'd gone out a few hours ago for fuel and to check on Kaelyn's family home. They'd expected him back before now. Grandma Joyce tried to call him, insisting he take his cell phone today, but the call wouldn't connect.

"Grandma," Kaelyn said as they sat down to eat, "do you think things will ever go back to normal?"

Grandma Joyce was quiet for a moment, stirring her soup thoughtfully. "I don't know, sweetheart. I hope so. But I think we might be looking at a new kind of normal for a while."

Kaelyn nodded, thinking about how quickly things had deteriorated. The local services, which had initially held up well, were starting to show signs of strain. Yesterday, the garbage truck hadn't come, and Grandpa Terry had muttered something about staff shortages.

The power had been flickering on and off, though nothing major yet, only brief outages, but enough to keep everyone on edge. The phones were hit or miss, with both cell phones and her grandparents' outdated landline unreliable. At least they'd heard from Kaelyn's parents by email a few times. They were fine, with no Star Bright incidents where they were. Kaelyn wondered how much longer they'd be able to stay in contact. The usually reliable internet sometimes wouldn't connect at all.

"Have you heard anything new from Mom and Dad?" she asked, though she already knew the answer.

Grandma Joyce shook her head. "Nothing since Sunday. I'd tell you if I did."

Kaelyn tried to push down the worry gnawing at her for days. She knew her grandmother was right. Logically, her parents were probably safe. But logic didn't stop the nightmares where she saw them singing that haunting tune, their eyes vacant and unfocused.

After lunch, Kaelyn helped clean up before retreating to her room. She pulled out her notebook, flipping through the pages of observations and theories she'd compiled. The Star Brights were still a mystery, but patterns were emerging. Almost all the incidents involved songs about stars, though the specific songs varied. The afflicted individuals seemed to enter a trance-like state before committing violent acts, and if they survived, they often had no memory of what they'd done.

A knock at her door interrupted her thoughts. "Come in," she called.

Grandpa Terry entered, his face grave. "Kaelyn, can you come downstairs? We want to talk with you."

"I didn't hear you come home. Is everything okay?"

"The rain has stopped for now." He shrugged. "That's something, I guess. Let's talk downstairs."

Heart racing, Kaelyn followed her grandfather to the living room. Her grandmother was already there, perched on the edge of the sofa.

"What's happened? Are my parents okay?"

Grandma Joyce shook her head. "We haven't heard anything."

"Earlier today, there was an incident at the hospital," Grandpa Terry said softly. "A nurse . . . well, let's say they're critically understaffed now. They're not even sure how they can tend to emergencies."

Kaelyn sank onto the couch, her mind reeling. The hospital. A nurse turned into a Star Bright? What would this mean for her cast? For her grandma's?

As if reading her thoughts, Grandma Joyce reached out and squeezed her hand. "We'll get through this, sweetheart. We need to be careful and look out for each other."

Kaelyn nodded, but she couldn't help but feel things were spiraling out of control. The safe, familiar Cody of her childhood seemed to be disappearing before her eyes, replaced by a town gripped by fear and suspicion. "Did everything else go okay? Did you have any trouble, Grandpa?"

"No trouble, not really. I saw a fight in the parking lot food line when I drove by, but I didn't stop to see what was going on. I stopped by your house, and all is well there. I brought some pantry items back with me. I don't think we should go to the food line unless it's absolutely necessary. I'll empty your house first. I've decided to take your mom's car and get fuel for it tomorrow. Your dad's day is Thursday, so I'll take his that day. We'll keep the cars here since it's smart to have extra vehicles available."

Her grandma's car was still in the parking lot at the Irma, a flattened lump of metal thanks to another car still resting on it. Even though Grandma Joyce had called their insurance and reported the trouble, nothing more had come of it. Insurance claims were not high on the list of priorities.

"How will we get the cars here?" her grandma asked, already shaking her head.

"I'm going to walk. It's only about a mile."

"I don't know . . ." She was still shaking her head. "I don't like you going around town. And walking . . . is that safe?"

"The only other option is one of you going with me, but with each of you laid up . . ."

"I could help you," Kaelyn offered. "My arm's feeling okay."

Her grandma shook her head. "I don't want Kaelyn to leave here unless she must."

"We'll figure it out," Grandpa Terry promised.

Later that evening, as they sat down to dinner, the power went out again. This time, it didn't flicker back on after a few seconds.

"I'll get the oil lamp." Grandpa Terry sighed.

"Eat, Terry. There's plenty of light coming in." Grandma Joyce motioned to the window, where it was still overcast outside and once again drizzling. "We'll get the lanterns later if we need them."

As they ate, Kaelyn couldn't help but think about how much had changed in only a week. The comfortable routines of small-town life had been shattered, replaced by a constant state of alertness and anxiety.

"Do you think we should leave?" she asked, surprising even herself with the question.

Her grandparents exchanged a look. "And go where, honey?" Grandma Joyce asked gently.

Kaelyn shrugged. "I don't know. Somewhere less populated maybe? Where there's less chance of . . . incidents."

Grandpa Terry shook his head. "For now, I think we're better off staying put. We have our home, our supplies, and we know the area. Besides, from what we've heard, the roads out of town can be difficult. Tourists trying to leave, locals trying to get in or out for supplies . . . it's not safe. Plus, with the fuel issues . . ."

Kaelyn nodded, understanding the logic but still feeling a pang of disappointment. Part of her had hoped they'd say yes. They'd pack up and drive off to somewhere untouched by the Star Bright phenomenon. But she knew it was wishful thinking. Nowhere seemed safe anymore.

As they cleaned up after dinner, working by the light of lanterns, Kaelyn's thoughts turned to her friends. She hadn't seen any of them since this all started. Text messages and social media had become their only form of communication, and even that was spotty with the increasingly unreliable internet.

Her best friend had sent a message yesterday, saying her family was thinking of leaving town. They had friends in Manderson, a much smaller town with a population of only a hundred, near the Bighorn Mountains. The news stirred both envy and fear in Kaelyn. Envy they might escape this nightmare and fear she might never see her friend again.

Her grandparents didn't think leaving was a good idea, but Kaelyn wasn't convinced. Maybe she could mention it again. She could make up a list of the pros and cons of leaving and they could discuss it. Even as she considered it, she knew making the list would be futile. It'd be like when she first presented her evidence of the connection between the Star Brights.

The power came back on as they were getting ready for bed, the sudden brightness making them all blink in surprise.

"Well, that's something at least," Grandpa Terry said with a note of forced cheerfulness in his voice.

As Kaelyn lay in bed that night, listening to the returning rain pattering against her window, she couldn't shake the feeling this was simply the beginning. The Star Brights, the fear, the breakdown of normal life—it all seemed like the opening chapters of a story she wasn't sure she wanted to finish.

But as she drifted off to sleep, one thought kept circling in her mind. They were still here. Still together. Still fighting. And as long as that was true, there was hope. It might be a different kind of normal, as Grandma Joyce had said, but it was something to hold on to in the darkness.

Tomorrow would bring new challenges and new fears to face. But for now, in the quiet of the night, Kaelyn allowed herself to believe they would find a way through this. Someday, somehow, the rain would stop, the sun would shine again, and Cody would once more be the town she knew and loved.

It was a small hope, perhaps a naive one. But in times like these, sometimes a small hope was all you had.

Chapter 8

The kitchen table was strewn with papers, Kaelyn's neat handwriting filling the lines with the pros and cons of leaving Cody. She tapped her pen against the *Cons* column, the biggest item catching her eye: *Where would we go?* The question loomed large, seeming to mock her efforts to find a solution.

Kaelyn glanced toward the living room where her grandmother dozed in the recliner, an open book resting on her lap. Grandma Joyce had said she was going to read, but Kaelyn suspected she hadn't slept well the night before. Come to think of it, Kaelyn hadn't slept great either.

She'd woken up around two in the morning to a noise downstairs. Heart pounding, she'd crept to the top of the stairs, only to see her grandmother moving about in the kitchen. Kaelyn had managed to fall back asleep eventually, but the incident left her feeling unsettled.

Grandpa Terry was out again, this time getting fuel for Kaelyn's mom's car. He'd left the house on foot while it was still dark. The thought of him walking and driving around town made her nervous, but she understood why he wanted to keep the cars filled. She tried to focus on her list, but her mind kept wandering to all the potential dangers lurking outside their home.

A sharp knock at the door made Kaelyn jump. She watched as her grandmother stirred, quickly moving to answer it. Standing on the porch was their pregnant neighbor, Chloe Beckwith, her face streaked with tears.

"I'm sorry," Chloe sobbed as Grandma Joyce ushered her inside. "I don't know who to turn to. My husband didn't come home last night. He went to pick up our food yesterday, and I can't reach him by phone. I don't know if . . . if something happened. But this isn't like him. He wouldn't— "

"There, there," Grandma Joyce soothed, guiding Chloe to the couch. "Come in. Let's see what we can do."

Chloe sank onto the cushions, her hands trembling. "I thought maybe I'd drive to the food drop. But, well, I hate to admit I'm scared to go out on my own. I was hoping maybe your husband . . ."

"He went to get fuel but should be back soon," Grandma Joyce explained.

"I could ride with you," Kaelyn offered, instantly regretting the words. The thought of leaving the safety of home sent a chill down her spine.

"No," her grandma said immediately, her tone leaving no room for disagreement. "Terry will be back soon."

They settled into an anxious wait, the ticking of the clock on the mantel seeming unnaturally loud in the tense silence. Kaelyn returned to her list but found it hard to concentrate with Chloe's quiet sobs filling the room.

Finally, they heard Grandpa Terry pull into the driveway. Grandma Joyce quickly explained the situation as he entered, a serious look settling over his weathered features.

"I'll help you," he said to Chloe. "Why don't . . . um, we might be a bit. Maybe go into the kitchen and get a drink of water? Kaelyn, can you help Chloe?"

"No, I'm ready to go," Chloe insisted, pushing herself to her feet.

Grandma Joyce smiled gently. "Get a drink. For your baby. You don't want to become dehydrated. Grab one of the water bottles to take with you too."

Kaelyn led Chloe to the kitchen, noticing the woman's impatience. She wasn't sure why her grandparents were insisting on this delay either, but she kept her thoughts to herself as she handed Chloe a water bottle.

When they returned to the living room, Grandma Joyce patted the spot next to her on the couch. "Can you have a seat, Chloe?"

"No, I'm ready to go," Chloe replied, frustration evident in her voice.

"Just for a minute. Please?" Her tone was gentle but insistent.

Chloe flopped down with a huff. Grandma Joyce sat next to her, placing a comforting hand on her arm. "Terry heard some news while he was in town. About trouble at the food drop yesterday. There were some injuries."

Chloe gasped, and her hand flew to her mouth. "My husband?"

Grandma Joyce squeezed her arm reassuringly. "He didn't get any names, but he is going to take you to the police department. They'll have info there, okay?"

Chloe nodded mutely, her face pale.

Grandpa Terry helped her to her feet, and they headed out to his truck.

As the door closed behind them, Kaelyn turned to her grandmother. "What's really going on?"

Her grandma sighed heavily. "Your grandpa heard it was bad. Several dead. It's probably the trouble he saw while driving by yesterday."

Kaelyn's stomach twisted. "But . . . maybe her husband was only among the injured?"

"Perhaps."

"Why didn't he call her?" Kaelyn pressed.

"I don't know. The phones don't work right. Maybe he lost his? I don't know. Let's pray. Pray for Chloe and whatever she may discover."

They sat together on the couch, heads bowed in silent prayer. Kaelyn found it hard to focus, her mind racing with possibilities. The world outside their door seemed to grow more dangerous by the day.

Hours passed before they heard Grandpa Terry's truck return. Kaelyn and her grandmother rushed to the door, their hearts sinking at the sight of Chloe's tear-stained face. The news was as bad as they'd feared. Her husband was among the dead.

Grandma Joyce immediately enveloped Chloe in a hug, murmuring words of comfort as she guided her inside. Kaelyn stood back, feeling helpless in the face of such grief.

"They said he didn't suffer," Chloe murmured. "Said he's in a better place. Why would they say that?"

Grandma Joyce shook her head.

"They also said I can't have a funeral. Not now, anyway. There're too many people dying. The funeral homes are overwhelmed, and they're keeping the bodies for now, but think they may have to dig one big grave to bury them all."

"The police told you this?"

"One of the sheriff deputies. He didn't sound too happy about it either but said they didn't have many options right now. Unless things change soon, that's what they're going to have to do. There's already been several hundred deaths in Cody, over a thousand in the county."

Eventually, Grandma Joyce took Chloe to the guest room, settling her into bed with promises to check on her soon.

When she returned, Grandpa Terry was waiting in the living room, his face tight with concern. "While I was out, my phone rang," he said.

Kaelyn's heart leaped. "My parents?"

"No, sorry." Her grandpa shook his head. "My friend Dick Reynolds. You know him, from church? He and his wife Ruth only attend about once a month. They have the lodge up by Yellowstone. East Gate Lodge and Cabins."

"Yes, I know him." Grandma Joyce nodded, while Kaelyn shrugged. She couldn't picture the man, but she knew his wife. She made amazing cinnamon rolls for the social time before church. While her cinnamon rolls were delicious, Kaelyn didn't dare speak to the woman. She always seemed to have a scowl on her face, which made Kaelyn feel uneasy and too nervous to strike up a conversation.

"He invited us to move up to the lodge, stay at his place until this blows over. They're not as affected by things. Fewer people, plus they have solar power and a big generator with a good supply of diesel. They're working together with the lodges on either side of them, forming an alliance, for security."

"Really?" Grandma Joyce's eyebrows rose in surprise. "Sounds smart."

"But . . . but I thought you said we wouldn't leave?" Kaelyn interjected, remembering her conversation from the night before. "I asked you last night about leaving."

Grandpa Terry nodded slowly. "Last night we didn't have any option but to stay here. Now . . ."

"We should talk about it," Grandma Joyce said softly. "Pray about it."

Kaelyn looked down at her unfinished pro/con list, then back at her grandparents. The idea of leaving Cody, the only home she'd ever known, filled her with a mixture of fear and hope. But as she thought about Chloe, grieving in their guest room, and all the other tragedies unfolding around them, she realized staying put might no longer be the safest option.

"Okay," she said, her voice barely above a whisper. "Let's talk about it. I've been thinking about how we should go. I've even made a list of pros and cons. I hate the idea of leaving your home and the garden. We've worked so hard on it—a con. But the biggest con was we didn't have anywhere to go. But now . . ."

"Now God has given us an option." Grandma Joyce's eyes were filled with tears. "Sometimes, we are guided to leave behind what we know and trust in the unknown. It's in these moments we find our true strength and purpose. We're not abandoning our home, Kaelyn. We're taking our memories and love with us, wherever we go."

"Your grandma's right, sweetheart. This reminds me of the story of Jacob in the Bible. There was a time when Jacob and his family were facing a great danger. Severe famine. They had to leave their home in Canaan and go to Egypt to survive. God guided Jacob, as He is guiding us now."

Grandpa Terry paused, his eyes thoughtful as he continued. "You see, Jacob didn't want to leave the land he knew, the land that held so many memories and promises. But God spoke to him, told him not to be afraid to go down to Egypt, because it was there He would make Jacob's family into a great nation. It wasn't abandoning his home; it was about survival and finding a new purpose. Like Jacob, we must trust this journey will take us where we need to be."

Grandpa gently squeezed Kaelyn's shoulder.

"We're not leaving behind our love and memories. We're taking all of that with us, and one day, we'll look back and see how this journey shaped us, made us stronger. So, let's have faith, as Jacob did, and trust we're being guided to a place of safety and growth."

Chapter 9

Kaelyn sat on the couch, her list of pros and cons gripped tightly in her hand. "I understand what you're saying, Grandma, Grandpa. It's just . . . everything feels so overwhelming right now. I'm scared of what's out there, of what's going to happen to us." She hesitated, looking down at her list. This was what she wanted. Why was she hesitating now?

She took a breath. "I want to believe, like Jacob did. I want to be brave and trust we're going to be okay. Letting go of what we're used to isn't easy." Her voice softened, filled with a mixture of fear and hope. "I'll try. I'll try to trust that going up to the Reynolds's lodge is the right choice."

"They have a garden. Even a greenhouse, if I remember correctly," Grandma Joyce said. "Maybe we can take some of the seedlings with us and replant them. Undoubtedly, we'll need to plant extra food for winter."

"Winter? Do you think we'll still be up there in winter?" Kaelyn's heart started beating funny. They had to be back in Cody and things had to return to normal before school started at the end of August. Her senior year of high school . . . she didn't want to miss that.

Grandma Joyce looked at Grandpa Terry, who shook his head. "I don't know, honey. I'd like to think the government will get a handle on this. Make a new vaccine they're talking about and stop this insanity. But . . ." He raised his hands. "The way I understand it, they don't even know what is causing people to act the way they are. Some doctors are saying it's a virus. Others say it's a bacteria.

They have to figure out what it is before they can make a cure. But what do I know? I'm only a paper pusher."

Kaelyn smiled at her grandpa. He always said that when referring to his job with the Bureau of Land Management in Cody. He retired years ago, when Kaelyn was still in elementary school, having reached his obligation.

"Kaelyn, honey," her grandma began, settling next to her on the couch. "We'd like to see the list you've been working on."

Kaelyn hesitated, her hand hovering over the papers. What if they thought her reasons were silly? What if she'd overlooked something crucial? Besides, what did her list really matter? It sounded like they'd already decided to leave. Taking a deep breath, she handed her list to her grandmother. "It's a bit disorganized," she mumbled, already regretting her decision to share it.

Grandma Joyce raised the list, her eyes scanning the neat columns. "Nonsense, dear. This looks very thorough."

Grandpa Terry leaned over his wife's shoulder, squinting slightly to read the small print. "Hmm, 'Pros: Safety in numbers, more resources, better security,'" he read aloud. "Those are good points."

A small flicker of pride sparked in Kaelyn, but doubt quickly extinguished it. "The cons are probably more important, though," she said quietly.

"Let's see," Grandma Joyce continued. "'Cons: Leaving our home, unknown situation, potential conflicts with strangers.' These are all valid concerns, Kaelyn."

"The biggest con was we didn't have a safe place to go," Kaelyn pointed out, tapping the paper. "But I guess that's changed now?"

Grandpa Terry nodded, pulling out a chair and sitting down. "Dick's place is pretty isolated. It's only a few miles from Yellowstone, which is completely shut down now. All the gates are closed."

"But couldn't people walk through?" Kaelyn asked, remembering their winter adventures. "Like when we go snowshoeing in the winter?"

"You're right," Grandma Joyce acknowledged. "People do hike into Yellowstone when it's closed during the winter. They could hike through now, but that's an awfully long way."

"True," Grandpa Terry agreed. "It could happen, but it's not likely to be many people. And I can't imagine they'd cause trouble, especially with the security setup Dick's planning with the other lodges."

Kaelyn nodded, but she felt uncertain. She was pretty sure she now knew who Dick Reynolds was, remembering him from church. While his wife was quiet and sometimes abrupt, Dick was friendly but loud, always cracking jokes Kaelyn found more awkward than funny.

As if reading her thoughts, Grandma Joyce added, "I know Dick can be a bit much sometimes. But he's a good man. His time in the military and running a machining shop in Douglas gave him a unique personality. He's mellowed some since moving to Cody."

Kaelyn was not entirely convinced. She knew her grandpa and Dick Reynolds had bonded over the fact they were both veterans, though her grandpa was Air Force and Dick was a Marine. They were friends, but were they good enough friends for something like this?

She wanted to believe this was the right decision, but doubt gnawed at her. What if they got there and it was terrible? What if Dick's jokes became unbearable? What if Ruth's abruptness turned into outright hostility?

"How would we even get there?" she asked, latching onto a practical concern. "We'd need a moving truck for all our stuff, wouldn't we?"

Grandpa Terry shook his head. "We'll only take the essentials. We can use my truck and your dad's truck. That should be enough space for what we need to take up to the lodge."

"Oh," Kaelyn said, deflating slightly. Part of her hoped the logistics might be too difficult, giving them a reason to stay. But deep down, she knew leaving was the right choice. Even though Cody wasn't terribly large, with a population of ten thousand—less now with the recent deaths—it was turning into something resembling a war zone.

"Something not on my list . . ." Kaelyn said, biting on her lip. "The rations. I guess I figured we'd go to another town, where we'd have rations. But if we move up by Yellowstone, there isn't a real town. Do you think they'll have something to help us with food?"

"Nope." Her grandpa shook his head. "I think that's one of the benefits. Look at Chloe's husband. He wasn't killed by one of those Star folks. He was killed when things fell apart in the ration line. The deputy told her he was trying to break up a fight between two others."

"That's terrible," Kaelyn whispered while Grandma Joyce shook her head.

"Yep. And I think it's only going to get worse. Until this whole disaster is over, we'll need to look over our shoulders, watching out for not only Star Brights but for people who we may have once called friends."

After several beats of silence, Grandma Joyce reached over and squeezed Kaelyn's hand. "What do you think, sweetie? Your opinion matters here."

Kaelyn's throat tightened. They were asking her what she thought, but what if she said the wrong thing? What if her decision put them all in danger? She opened her mouth, then closed it again, unsure of what to say.

"It's okay if you don't know," Grandpa Terry said softly. "This is a big decision."

Kaelyn nodded, grateful for the understanding. "I . . . I think it might be good to go," she said hesitantly. "But I'm also scared. What if it doesn't work out?"

"That's a valid fear," Grandma Joyce reassured her. "But sometimes we have to take risks to stay safe. And we'll be together, which is the most important thing."

As Kaelyn processed that, her grandma's expression changed. "Oh! We should ask Chloe if she wants to come with us. The poor dear is all alone now, and she couldn't reach her family or her husband's family on the phone. They don't live in Wyoming. His folks are somewhere back east, and hers are in Colorado. I can't imagine she'd be able to get to them."

Grandpa Terry frowned slightly. "I suppose if she wants to go. I don't think Dick would mind, as long as she pulls her weight. He mentioned everyone has to work. There's a security watch schedule, and they all pitch in around the place. They've got a garden, chickens, a few cattle, and they're working on securing more livestock."

"Was Chloe with you when Dick called?" Grandma Joyce asked.

"No, she was back with the officer. I'll tell you, when my phone rang, it about scared it all out of me. I was surprised Dick got through. He was too. Said he'd tried a dozen times over the last few days."

Kaelyn listened to the exchange, her mind whirling with new possibilities and concerns. The idea of Chloe joining them was both comforting and anxiety-inducing. On one hand, it would be nice to have someone else along, especially someone who might need their help. On the other hand, what if Chloe's grief made the journey more difficult? What if she changed her mind halfway there?

"Do you think Chloe would *want* to come?" Kaelyn asked, her voice small.

Grandma Joyce smiled gently. "We won't know unless we ask her. But it's the right thing to offer, don't you think?"

Kaelyn nodded, feeling a range of emotions she couldn't quite sort out. The idea of leaving Cody, the only home she'd ever known, filled her with a deep sadness. But staying put no longer felt safe. The Star Brights were everywhere, and no one knew when or where the next incident would occur.

"If . . . if we go," Kaelyn started, then paused, gathering her courage. "If we go, how soon would we leave?"

Grandpa Terry exchanged a look with Grandma Joyce before answering. "Well, we'd need to pack, of course. And make sure both trucks are fueled up. Mine is fine. Tomorrow is the day we can get our two gallons for your dad's truck. I plan to be in line early to get that done. I'd say we could be ready by tomorrow afternoon if we push it."

"Tomorrow?" Kaelyn's eyes widened. It seemed so soon, so final.

"The sooner we go, the safer it'll be," Grandma Joyce said. "The roads are still passable now, but who knows how long it'll last?"

Kaelyn glanced down at her list, the pros and cons seeming inadequate in the face of this massive decision. She wanted to be brave, to embrace this change as an adventure, but fear kept creeping in.

"What about Mom and Dad?" she asked. "What if they are able to get home and we're not here?"

Grandpa Terry's voice gentled. "I think it'd be a miracle if they were somehow able to get home. But we'll send them an email if we can. And we could leave a note at their house. And Dick's place has a phone that still works sometimes. After all, he did call me. We can keep trying to reach them, let them know where we are."

"Okay." She wanted to say more, to express all the conflicting emotions swirling inside her, but the words wouldn't come.

Her grandma moved around the table to wrap her in a hug. "It's okay to be scared, sweetheart. We all are."

Kaelyn leaned into the embrace, drawing comfort from her grandmother's warmth. She wanted to believe everything would be okay, that this was the right decision. But doubt still lingered, whispering worst-case scenarios in the back of her mind.

"Should we go talk to Chloe now?" Grandpa Terry glanced toward the guest room.

Grandma Joyce nodded. "Yes, I think that would be best. If she's awake."

"Thought I heard some moving around back there." Grandpa Terry pointed toward the hallway.

"Kaelyn, would you like to come with us?" her grandma asked as she stood.

She hesitated. Part of her wanted to stay in the living room, to pore over her list again and again, searching for some clear answer. But she knew no amount of list-making would change the reality of their situation. The decision had been made. They were leaving Cody. She should be happy. After all, that was what she wanted, wasn't it?

"Okay," she said finally, standing up. "I'll come."

As they walked toward the guest room, a storm of questions swirled in Kaelyn's head. *How will Chloe react to our offer? Will she want to come with us? And if she does, how will that change the dynamic of our small group, of our family?*

Grandma Joyce knocked on the guest room door. "Chloe? Are you awake, dear? We'd like to talk to you about something important."

There was a moment of silence, then a quiet "Come in" from the other side of the door.

As they entered the room, Kaelyn hung back slightly, unsure of her place in this conversation. She watched as her grandparents explained the situation to Chloe, outlining Dick's offer and extending the invitation for her to join them.

Chloe's eyes, red-rimmed from crying, widened in surprise. "You . . . you want me to come with you?" she asked, her voice hoarse.

"Only if you want to, dear," Grandma Joyce assured her. "We thought, with everything that's happened . . . well, we don't want to leave you alone."

Chloe's lower lip trembled, and for a moment, Kaelyn thought she might start crying again. But then she took a deep breath and squared her shoulders. "I . . . I think I'd like to go with you. If you're sure I won't be a burden."

"Not at all," Grandpa Terry said firmly. "Although there may be some tough days ahead. We'll all be working together to survive."

As the others continued to discuss the logistics of their departure, Kaelyn found herself drifting to the window.

She gazed out at the familiar landscape of their backyard, the vegetable garden her grandparents had so lovingly tended, the old tire swing hanging from the big oak tree, planted years ago when they'd first bought the place. The tire was added for her dad and her uncle to use. Would she ever see that view again?

A lump formed in her throat. They were leaving Cody, venturing into an uncertain future. Part of her wanted to protest, to beg her grandparents to reconsider. But she knew, deep down, this was their best chance of survival.

Still, as she turned back to the room, watching her grandparents comfort Chloe and discuss plans for their journey, Kaelyn couldn't shake the feeling of being adrift. Everything was changing so fast, and she felt woefully unprepared for what lay ahead.

She wanted to be strong, to face this new challenge with courage and determination. But as she stood there, silent and uncertain, Kaelyn couldn't help but wonder, was she ready for this? Could she leave it all behind and face the unknown?

The questions swirled in her mind, unanswered and daunting. But as her grandmother caught her eye and offered a reassuring smile, Kaelyn managed a small nod in return. At the request of his son Joseph, Jacob took a chance and left everything he knew to go to Egypt in order for the family to survive the famine.

While what was happening now was certainly different, and Kaelyn wasn't a Biblical hero, survival was survival. She took a deep breath, steeling herself for the journey ahead.

Chapter 10

Kaelyn's fingers fumbled with the zipper on her bag as she glanced around her cluttered bedroom. She stood back, surveying the small pile of belongings she'd gathered. A sense of purpose filled her, pushing aside the doubts that had plagued her earlier. They were doing the right thing. She was sure of it now.

Soon, she and her grandparents would be secure at the Reynolds's lodge. It felt right, biblical as her grandparents had said. Like Jacob, they were venturing into the unknown, trusting in God's guidance.

"Ready to head over to your place?" Grandpa Terry's voice broke through her reverie.

Kaelyn nodded. "I still have some packing to do, but I've got things sorted. It'll be easier to finish when I get the rest of my stuff from my house. And another suitcase or two."

"We'll see what we can fit. Our space is limited, and we'll want to make sure the things we take are all useful items."

"I understand."

They climbed into her mom's car, the familiar scent of leather and her mother's favorite air freshener bringing a lump to Kaelyn's throat.

As they pulled out of the driveway, Grandpa Terry sighed. "Couldn't get through to Dick. Phone lines must be acting up again. But it'll be fine. They're expecting us. I don't think they'll mind that we're bringing Chloe along."

"I tried to get ahold of my parents and couldn't reach them either. The internet is also not working right."

"Don't worry about your folks. I'm sure they're fine. There hasn't been much mention of trouble where they are."

She agreed with a nod. Her parents were safe, far from the trouble engulfing their hometown and much of the world. On the increasingly rare occasion the internet worked, Kaelyn checked for updates to see if there were any new reports. While there had been issues in some of the more populated areas of Africa, it didn't seem to affect the lesser-populated area where her parents were working on the school.

Hopefully, the virus hadn't reached them and wouldn't. Of course, she knew that may be wishful thinking. She understood how viruses spread.

But as her grandpa had said, the doctors and scientists weren't entirely sure how the Star Bright affliction was spreading. Was it a virus or some kind of bacteria? Was it airborne, or did it travel in a different way, maybe through contact or bodily fluids? No one seemed to know. But she liked to think her parents would remain safe where they were, and when it was contained, they'd return home.

The drive to Kaelyn's house was short but tense. The streets were quiet, with only a few people hurrying along the sidewalks, heads down and shoulders hunched. Kaelyn was glad when they finally pulled into her driveway.

Inside, they worked efficiently, gathering shelf-stable food from the pantry and kitchen cabinets.

"Let's take what we can from the freezer," her grandpa said. "We'll put it in our freezer and then pack as much as we can to take with us. We've got a couple of good-sized coolers that should keep things frozen until we get up to the Reynolds's place."

After they finished with the food, Kaelyn's eyes moved to the family photos on the walls and the little knickknacks that made the place home. She swallowed hard, pushing down the emotions threatening to overwhelm her.

She decided she'd take a couple of photos with her, pulling them from their frames to make them easier to carry: one from her parents' wedding, another of the three of them when she was just a few months old, and an old photo of her dad with his late brother before leukemia took him at age ten.

"Don't forget your winter clothes," Grandpa Terry reminded her as she headed upstairs. "And grab your parents' gear too. Snowshoes, skis—the whole lot."

Kaelyn paused on the stairs. "You think we'll need all that?"

"Hope for the best, prepare for the worst. If we're home before the snow flies, great. If not, well, we'll be glad to have it."

"Some of those things are kept in the garage."

"I'll take care of finding them. Get your parents' clothes, okay?"

"Why?"

"Better to have it. Might come in handy."

Nodding, Kaelyn continued upstairs to her room. She packed quickly, grabbing warm layers, heavy boots, and the winter sports equipment. As she worked, her eyes fell on her bookshelf. On impulse, she grabbed her favorite novels and her most recent school yearbook, tucking them into her bag.

In her parents' room, she took several minutes to look around before taking her mom's large suitcase from the closet. They'd taken smaller carry-on size bags with them, saying they wouldn't need much since they'd basically wear the same clothes each day. Kaelyn wasn't exactly sure why her grandpa thought bringing her parents' clothes was necessary, but she didn't have it in her to argue.

Back downstairs, they added a few more items to their growing pile—a toolkit, first aid supplies, batteries, and flashlights. Grandpa Terry insisted on bringing the family's emergency radio and solar charger.

"I'm sure Dick has things like this, but it's still smart to bring our own. You never know when information might be crucial," he said, carefully wrapping the devices.

They also packed some basic camping gear—sleeping bags, a small tent, and cooking supplies. Her dad was an avid outdoorsman, and she was grateful now for his preparedness.

As they loaded the car, she realized they'd need to make a second trip. The vehicle was packed to the brim, with barely enough room for them to sit, and they were only halfway finished.

"We'll come back for the rest," Grandpa Terry said, closing the trunk with a grunt. "Let's get this load home first."

The return trip was uneventful, and they quickly unloaded at her grandparents' house. Grandma Joyce helped, creating an efficient assembly line from the car to their house. Chloe was at her house, working on getting her things together.

They were about halfway back to her house when Grandpa Terry slowed the car. "Look," he said quietly, nodding toward the end of the street.

Kaelyn's eyes widened as she took in the scene. A group of people were gathered outside the Army Recruiting

Station, their voices raised in angry shouts. As she watched, someone threw a rock, shattering one of the store's windows.

"What's happening?" Kaelyn whispered, her heart racing.

"Craziness," her grandpa muttered, his expression hard. "Someone's not happy about something."

"Are they all Star Brights?"

"Doubtful. My guess is they're simply upset Wyomingites. You've heard about the governor's heavy-handed tactics with Cheyenne and Casper? There's concern he'll order the National Guard to do similar things here in Cody. Some of the other larger towns too. One rumor is every town over ten thousand."

"I heard, but we were barely over that before the Star Brights. And now we're less."

"Right. But we do still have tourists here, people who either couldn't get home or decided to stay for some reason."

He accelerated, passing by the riot. "We're going to make a quick detour on the way home. You know my friend Von Weddle? I'm going to swing by his place."

"Why?"

"When I was talking with Dick, he said to let him know if I thought of people who might be an asset. We talked about Von. I want to see if Dick was able to get ahold of him." He slowed as they neared the street to Kaelyn's home. "Maybe we should go to Von's first? Not drive around with the car full."

As he sped up, Kaelyn shrugged and stared out the window. Von Weddle and his wife, whose name Kaelyn couldn't remember but was some kind of flower, also went to the same church as they did. They both seemed nice enough and, like her grandparents, were of retirement age.

They pulled up in front of the modest home. As her grandpa put the car into park, Kaelyn asked, "Should I wait here?"

Shaking his head, he told her he wasn't comfortable with her staying in the car. It was several minutes after they rang the doorbell before they heard, "Terry Fisher? Who's with you?"

Kaelyn shifted her gaze to the doorbell camera and tried to smile while her grandpa moved in front of the peephole. "It's me. Kaelyn, my granddaughter, is with me."

The door opened only a few inches. "What can I do for you?" The gruff male voice asked.

With a furrowed brow, her grandpa said, "I'm not one of those stupid Star Brights, Von."

"Well, how do I know? You may be infected and— "

"I'm not infected. Neither is Kaelyn. Look, if you're worried, then we'll be on our way."

The door opened wider, revealing Von Weddle, a tall man with graying hair and a weathered face. He looked apologetic but still wary.

"I'm sorry, Terry. Can't be too careful these days. What brings you by?"

"No offense taken. Listen, have you heard from Dick Reynolds lately?"

Von shook his head. "No, can't say that I have. Why do you ask?"

"Dick called me. He's invited us to move up to his lodge near Yellowstone. Says it's safer up there, and they're forming a sort of community with the neighboring lodges."

Von's eyebrows raised in interest. "Is that so?"

"Yeah. I thought you and Daisy might want to consider coming along. It'd probably be safer than staying in town, given how things are deteriorating."

Von rubbed his chin thoughtfully. "It's certainly something to consider. Daisy and I have been worried about the situation here."

Terry nodded. "We're planning to leave tomorrow at one. If you decide you want to join us, be packed and ready. We'll meet at the church, but we can only wait until one fifteen. After that, we've got to get on the road."

Von glanced back into his house, then turned to Terry. "I appreciate the offer, Terry. Daisy and I will discuss it and make a decision. If we decide to go, we'll be there."

"All right. I hope to see you there, but I understand if you choose to stay. Take care, Von."

"You too, Terry. And you, Kaelyn," Von added with a nod to her.

As they walked back to the car, Kaelyn couldn't help but wonder if they'd see the Weddles at the church tomorrow. She climbed into the passenger seat as her grandfather started the engine.

They soon made it to Kaelyn's house and loaded the car. Like the first time, it was a tight fit, but they were able to get in everything they wanted to bring. As they drove home, Kaelyn couldn't shake the image of the angry crowd. Cody, the town she'd known and loved all her life, was becoming unrecognizable. The realization hit her hard. They were no longer safe here. She'd known that before, but it was still hard to accept.

Back at her grandparents' house, Grandma Joyce was waiting on the porch. Her face lit up with relief as they pulled in.

"Thank goodness you're back," she said, hurrying down the steps. "Chloe's over at her place, packing. Kaelyn, why don't you go give her a hand? The poor dear seems a bit overwhelmed."

Kaelyn nodded, grateful for the distraction. She found Chloe in her bedroom, surrounded by piles of clothes, looking lost.

"Need some help?" Kaelyn asked.

Chloe looked up, her eyes red-rimmed. "I don't even know where to start."

Kaelyn stepped in and took charge. "Let's do what we did at my place. We'll start with the kitchen and bathroom, then tackle clothes and any important items you want to bring."

Working together, they made quick progress. Kaelyn helped Chloe sort through her wardrobe, focusing on sturdy, practical clothes and warm layers for winter. They packed toiletries, medications, and a few cherished mementos.

As they worked, Chloe began to open up, sharing stories about her husband and their plans for the baby. Kaelyn listened, offering quiet support and the occasional hug when Chloe's emotions overwhelmed her.

By the time they finished, the sun was setting. They carried Chloe's belongings over to her grandparents' house, loading them into Grandpa Terry's truck in the garage.

Exhausted but satisfied with their progress, they all gathered in the kitchen for a simple dinner of canned soup and crackers. As they ate, Grandpa Terry outlined the plan for the next day.

"I'll take your mom's car back to your place in the morning," he said to Kaelyn. "Switch it out for your dad's pickup. I'll go get our fuel allotment. Two gallons. It's not much, but with what's already in the rig, it should be enough to get us to the lodge."

He paused, taking a sip of water. "My truck's right about three-quarters full, and your dad's is about the same. We'll load them both up. They've got those tonneau covers, so we can stack things pretty high in the bed. Plus, we can use the back seats for more storage."

Chloe spoke up, her voice stronger than it had been all day. "I can drive the second truck. I'm used to handling big vehicles."

Grandpa Terry nodded approvingly. "Good. Kaelyn, you'll ride with Chloe. Grandma and I will take the lead in my truck." He paused for a moment as he thought. "If Von and Daisy decide to go, I'll have him take the lead. He's been up to the lodge plenty of times too. You two will be in the middle, and we'll bring up the rear."

As they discussed the final details, a surge of confidence washed over Kaelyn. They had a solid plan, plenty of supplies, and they were all working together. She felt a rush of hope. Maybe they weren't leaving Canaan for Egypt as Jacob had done, but it felt nearly the same. It felt like a chance for safety. A chance to escape the catastrophe surrounding them.

"All right," Grandpa Terry said, pushing back from the table. "I think we're as ready as we'll ever be. Let's pray God will be with us on this journey."

Kaelyn bowed her head as he began to pray. "Lord, we come before You in this time of uncertainty and fear. We ask for Your protection as we embark on this journey. Guide us, shield us from harm, and grant us the strength and wisdom to face whatever challenges lie ahead. Like Jacob of old, we're leaving our home in search of safety.

Be with us, Lord, as You were with him. In Jesus's name, amen."

"Amen," the Fishers echoed. Chloe stared at her hands resting in her lap.

Later, as Kaelyn prepared for bed, a sense of peace settled over her. Tomorrow would bring new challenges. No matter what came next, she trusted that God would lead them.

Chapter 11

The low rumble of the pickup's engine filled the cab as Kaelyn and Chloe made their way through Cody's deserted streets. Gray clouds hung low, threatening another round of rain and matching the somber mood inside the vehicle. Kaelyn fidgeted with her seatbelt, stealing glances at Chloe's tight-lipped profile.

The silence between them was heavy, broken only by the occasional sniffle from Chloe. Kaelyn grasped for words of comfort, but nothing she thought of seemed enough in the face of such a profound loss.

As they approached the church, Chloe finally spoke. Her voice was raw, barely above a whisper. "What's the point of all this? A loving God wouldn't let this happen."

Kaelyn's breath caught in her throat. She'd grown up in this church, its teachings a cornerstone of her life. She was supposed to be in East Africa right now, helping her parents build a school and share God's love. They'd taken classes on how to spread the Gospel, but nothing had prepared her for this.

"I . . . I don't know," Kaelyn admitted, her voice small. She turned to look out the window, watching raindrops spatter against the glass. What could she say to a woman who had lost everything?

Von's truck was idling in the church parking lot. Daisy sat rigidly in the driver's seat, her face a mask of worry. Grandpa Terry's pickup pulled in behind them, completing their small convoy.

They gathered briefly, Von and Grandpa Terry shaking hands while the rest of them got out of the vehicles. Daisy held a box of walkie-talkies.

"We thought these would be good for staying in contact. Easier than the phones."

Von's voice was gruff as he pointed first at Grandma Joyce and then at Kaelyn. "You didn't mention Joyce was injured. Or that your granddaughter would be in a third vehicle. Her dad's truck, right?" He turned to Chloe. "And you are?"

"Chloe Beckwith," she muttered, not bothering to meet Von's stern gaze.

"I don't think I know you."

"Chloe is our neighbor. Her husband . . ." Grandma Joyce shook her head, letting the words fade. "She'll be joining us at Dick's lodge."

Von pierced Grandpa Terry with a look. "Seems this is some info I should have been given when you stopped by my place."

He lifted his hands. "It didn't occur to me."

"How do you see this happening? I figured you and I'd be taking watch," he patted the pistol on his hip. "I've got a shotgun and rifle in the truck. Thought we'd let the women drive."

Shaking his head, her grandpa said, "I'm not sure Joyce can drive with her wrist the way it is. She's still in some pain. And Kaelyn's cast is pretty cumbersome."

"I can drive," Kaelyn said, sounding less than sure.

Von scoffed. "Daisy and I will take the lead. I guess I'll have to act as security for the lot of you." He pointed to Grandpa Terry's hip. "At least you're armed. I suppose you can shoot with one hand and drive with the other."

"You know full well I can handle a pistol, too, Von Fisher." Grandma Joyce's tone left no room for doubt. "Terry worked with me last night to use the door frame of the truck as a brace when shooting my .357."

Von exhaled, his expression showing a trace of apology. "I'm sure you'll do what's needed. I just . . . these are things we should have discussed. I understand it's partly my fault." He shifted his gaze to Grandpa Terry. "I was less than welcoming yesterday. It's hard to know who you can trust with the way things are. Our next-door neighbor turned out to be one of those crazies. He killed his wife and kids before killing himself."

"The former mayor?" Grandma Joyce shook her head. "That neighbor?"

"Yep, that neighbor." Von nodded. "It was pretty terrible."

"We hadn't heard," Grandpa Terry said. "I'm sorry."

"Yeah. Me too. I didn't agree with his politics, but he was a nice enough guy, even if he was glued to his computer most of the day. It's not like it used to be, where people worked with their hands." Von raised his calloused hands, the knuckles rough and scarred, dirt stubbornly clinging to the creases.

Kaelyn glanced at her grandpa's hands. Even though he'd spent the latter part of his career in an office, his early years had been spent in the field, doing work she wasn't entirely sure about but knew he loved. Since retiring, he had taken up countless hobbies to keep himself busy—the garden, a small woodworking shop in the shed, and an array of other projects. All that labor had left his hands weathered and worn, much like Von's.

Von looked at Chloe and then Kaelyn. "I suppose with them in the middle of our little convoy, they'll be somewhat safe."

Grandma Joyce rested her hand on Kaelyn's shoulder. "Terry worked with them too. Kaelyn's comfortable shooting, having gone deer and antelope hunting for the last several years with her folks. She can't handle the rifle right now, but she's good with a pistol. Aren't you, dear?"

Kaelyn shrugged one shoulder in response. While it was true, her grandpa had worked with all three women the night before, teaching them to shoot if necessary, they hadn't used live ammunition. She had shot a handgun before, several times in fact. Last year, after sighting in the rifles for hunting season, they had spent some time practicing with them.

Her dad always carried what he called his bear gun while hunting, and her mom carried a shotgun loaded in some special way Kaelyn didn't fully understand. It was designed to stop a grizzly. Her mom also wore a revolver on her hip, acting as protection rather than hunting.

Their firearms, along with her dad's archery equipment and other hunting gear, were securely packed in the truck bed. Kaelyn now carried her mom's .357 Magnum revolver, loaded with .38 Special rounds. Her grandpa said the recoil would be lighter that way, and she knew from last year's target practice he was right.

Chloe was also comfortable shooting and had a collection of guns belonging either to her or her husband. While most were packed away in the back of the truck, there was a rifle and pistol in the cab, along with Kaelyn's revolver.

"Well, I guess we'll have to make do. We'll take the lead. You two in the middle, and Terry bringing up the rear. Stay close, and don't stop for anything."

"Shall we pray?" Grandpa Terry asked, reaching for Kaelyn's hand. Chloe shook her head and walked back to the truck.

"What's wrong with her?" Von asked, taking his wife's hand.

"She's grieving," Grandma Joyce said simply.

After asking for God's blessing on their journey, Grandma Joyce pulled Kaelyn into a hug. "We'll be up at the lodge before we know it." She smiled. "I know this is scary, but I'm feeling confident this is the right thing for us to do. You'll be safe there."

"We'll all be safe there, right?"

She met Kaelyn's gaze. "Whatever happens, your safety is what's important. You and Chloe are to stay right on Von's bumper. Don't worry about anything else. If, for some reason, Von and Daisy can't continue, you and Chloe must. You know where the lodge is, so make sure you get there."

A sinking feeling filled Kaelyn's stomach. "Why are you talking like this?"

Kissing her on the cheek, she said, "You know how much I love you? How much light you've brought to my life? To your grandpa's life? All that matters is your safety. Chloe and you must keep going, no matter what. Promise me you will."

Kaelyn nodded, her stomach churning with both fear and anticipation. "Okay, we will. But you will, too, right? We'll stay on Von's bumper, and you'll stay on ours? Then we'll all get to the lodge."

"That's right." Her grandma pulled her close again. "We'll see you soon."

Before they parted, Daisy handed each truck one of the walkie-talkies, telling them it was already on and set to the correct frequency.

As they climbed back into their vehicles, she caught a glimpse of her grandmother's reassuring smile from the passenger seat of her grandpa's truck. It steadied her, if only for a moment.

The town Kaelyn had known all her life was now a shadow of itself. As they drove, she took in the boarded-up storefronts and the abandoned cars lining the streets. Restaurant windows were shattered, remnants picked clean by desperate looters.

When they drove by the Irma, Kaelyn craned her neck to catch a glimpse of her grandma's car still in the parking lot with another car resting on it.

"I heard you were there when it happened," Chloe said.

"We were," she replied, her voice sounding hollow to her ears.

They passed the hospital, its parking lot a sea of large tents. People huddled under blankets, their faces gaunt and fearful. A harried-looking woman hurried between the tents, her scrubs splattered with what Kaelyn hoped was only mud.

The museum parking lot was suspiciously empty of cars, but Kaelyn noticed several people pacing around the front, all well-armed. She'd heard plans had been put in place to protect the museum and the rich history it provided. While she knew the place was important to the town and the region, she wondered if all that manpower was truly necessary.

The Cody Stampede Rodeo Grounds, home of the nightly summer rodeo, loomed ahead. Kaelyn knew this was one of the places being used to pass out the food rations. She was surprised to see less of a crowd waiting there than they'd had at the parking lot where Grandpa Terry picked up their food. Of course, he hadn't gone back since Chloe's husband was killed. Maybe the lines were less there now too.

Maybe people were too scared to go out.

As they passed a former restaurant turned event rental location, the familiar smell of sulfur wafted through the open windows. Her grandpa had insisted she ride with her window down and her pistol handy, paying attention to not only what she could see outside but also what she could hear.

Thinking of her grandpa's instructions brought her back to the weird way Grandma Joyce was acting. Was she concerned about the trip up to the lodge? She didn't seem scared, not exactly, but more like she wanted to impress upon Kaelyn how reaching the lodge was the most important thing. There was a resigned quality in her demeanor, as if she understood something deeper about the journey ahead.

Chloe made a face. "I'll never get used to that smell."

"Stinking Water," Kaelyn replied. "That's what John Colter originally called the Shoshone River."

"He was right. My husband said there used to be a public hot spring, but it closed years ago." She let out a sigh. "He loved living here. He thought Cody was the perfect town to raise a family. I would have been happy to remain in Gillette, but when he was offered work here . . ." Chloe's voice faded away as she tightened her jaw. Her attempts to control her emotions failed, and a tear trickled down her cheek.

They drove on in silence, Kaelyn gazing out the window, her eyes drawn to the river. This area was undeniably beautiful. Up ahead, a road led to a popular hiking trail, one she and her parents especially loved in winter. During the colder months, the river transformed into something almost magical, its surface partially frozen in a striking shade of blue-green, like a gemstone catching the light.

As they crossed over a bridge, the road took a slight corner. The crack of gunfire shattered the tranquil scene. Kaelyn's heart leaped into her throat as she saw figures emerging from behind abandoned cars and rock formations, weapons raised.

"Get down!" Chloe screamed, slamming her foot on the accelerator. The truck lurched forward, engine roaring.

Kaelyn ducked, trying to make herself as small as possible, while searching for the shooters, revolver in her hand. Could her gun do any good in this situation? Through the windshield, she saw Von's truck fishtail as he swerved to avoid a makeshift barricade. Sparks flew from his back wheel. Had they hit his tire?

The truck bounced violently as Chloe maneuvered around debris in the road. Kaelyn's stomach churned, her breath coming in short, panicked gasps. She glanced in the side mirror, desperate to see her grandparents' truck.

"Are they okay?" she yelled over the din of gunfire and screeching tires.

Chloe didn't answer; her focus was entirely on the road ahead as she weaved through the mess. Kaelyn's eyes widened in horror as she saw a figure leap toward their truck, rifle aimed directly at them. The first bullet hit the windshield, causing it to spider crack.

Chloe swerved toward him. There was a sickening thud as she clipped him with the bumper, sending him up and over the top of the cab. She swerved again. Kaelyn watched in the side mirror as the man landed on the pavement. She thought she could even hear the thud of his body hitting the ground.

"Please, God, please help us," Kaelyn whimpered. She caught sight of another attacker as he emerged from behind a boulder. With what she knew was terrible aim, she squeezed the trigger of her gun, the recoil jolting her hand. She doubted her bullet had found its mark, but the assailant hesitated before retreating out of sight.

Just then, a bullet shattered the side mirror, sending shards of glass flying into the cab and forcing Kaelyn to flinch away from the sudden explosion of danger. She felt a sharp sting on her cheek and the warm trickle of blood.

Chloe cursed, hunching lower over the steering wheel as she pushed the truck to its limits.

Kaelyn's mind raced with terrifying possibilities. What if they didn't make it? What if her grandparents were hit? The thought of losing them, of being alone in this nightmare world, was almost too much to bear.

The gunfire ended as fast as it began. Kaelyn cautiously raised her head, her heart pounding so hard she thought it might burst from her chest. She looked back, relief flooding through her as she saw her grandparents' truck still following, though a plume of steam billowed from under the hood.

Chloe's face was a mask of determination, tears streaming down her cheeks as she kept pace with Von's vehicle. The older man's truck limped along, one wheel throwing up a shower of sparks with each rotation.

They rounded a bend, and the mouth of the first of a series of three tunnels loomed before them. Would the tunnels be safe, or was there another ambush waiting for them?

Kaelyn held her breath as they plunged into the near darkness, the echoes of their engines amplified in the confined space. Her hands gripped the dashboard so tightly that her knuckles turned white.

Emerging on the other side, Kaelyn blinked in the sudden brightness. The second short tunnel appeared almost immediately, and they quickly entered it, the darkness swallowing them again for a brief moment.

As they exited the second tunnel, the long third tunnel stretched out before them. The tunnel lights flickered, casting unsettling shadows on the walls. Kaelyn's heart raced as they drove in, the dim light playing tricks on her eyes. The mountain hung over them, the engine noise echoing through the extended tunnel, with sparks from Von's truck briefly lighting the area.

She turned in her seat to peer out the back window, relieved to see her grandparents' truck following closely. Kaelyn tilted her head as she tried to make out what she was seeing.

Instead of being on the passenger's side, Grandma Joyce was more in the middle of the seat, leaning against Grandpa Terry. She kept her gaze on her grandparents as she counted the seconds, each one dragging out as they drove deeper into the tunnel.

Finally, a faint light appeared, growing brighter as they neared the exit. Bursting into the open air, Kaelyn exhaled deeply, her eyes adjusting to the light once more.

Von's brake lights flashed and his left turn signal alerted as they neared the parking lot of Buffalo Bill Dam Visitor Center.

"Do we stop?" Chloe asked, slowing the truck. Kaelyn glanced again behind them to see her grandpa's turn signal also flashing. The radio sounded. It was her grandpa, telling them to pull into the lot.

Chloe followed Von, bringing their truck to a shuddering stop beside him. Before the vehicle had fully settled, Kaelyn was out the door, stumbling on shaky legs toward her grandparents' truck.

"Grandma! Grandpa!" she called, her voice cracking.

The driver's side window went down, and Grandpa Terry called to her, his face ashen. "Kaelyn," he said, his voice hollow.

She ran to him, stopping just shy of the door. "Are you okay? Grandma?"

"Kaelyn," he said again, his voice breaking as he shook his head. "Your grandmother . . . she . . ."

Kaelyn pulled back, looking up into her grandfather's tear-filled eyes. "No," she whispered, shaking her head. "No, no, no."

Chapter 12

Kaelyn rushed around to the other side of the truck and yanked open the passenger door. Grandma Joyce sat slumped in her seat, still leaning against Grandpa Terry's shoulder, her eyes closed as if in sleep. But the dark stain spreading across her floral blouse told a different story.

"Grandma?" Her voice was small, childlike. She reached out with trembling fingers to touch her grandma's hand. It was warm and soft, but terrifyingly still.

A heart-wrenching wail tore from Kaelyn's throat, a sound of pure anguish that bounced off the canyon walls and rippled across Buffalo Bill Reservoir. Daisy's arms closed around her, intending to guide her away from the truck, but Kaelyn fought against her, desperate to wake her grandmother from her impossible sleep.

"Let her stay," Grandpa Terry said. "Let her say goodbye."

"You're sure?" Daisy loosened her grip, and Kaelyn moved toward the truck—slower this time, cautious.

"It's okay," he murmured, gently touching his wife's hair, his own voice thick with grief. "Come on and say your goodbyes."

Kaelyn collapsed against her grandma, her body shaking with sobs. She barely registered the others gathering around them.

Daisy had stepped back to stand beside her husband, Von, both of their faces etched with shock as they kept watch on the truck and stayed ready to respond to any new threat.

Chloe lingered close by, clutching her rifle, tears streaming down her face.

Time seemed to lose all meaning as Kaelyn clung to her grandmother, her world crumbling around her. Her grandfather's rough hand patted her shoulder. *How can this be happening? How can Grandma Joyce be gone? The woman who taught me to bake, who kissed away my scraped knees, who had always been a pillar of strength and love. How could she be gone?*

Memories flooded Kaelyn's mind—Grandma Joyce's laugh as they worked in the garden, her gentle hands braiding Kaelyn's hair for church, her wise words of advice when Kaelyn had her first heartbreak. Each memory was a fresh stab of pain, a reminder of all she'd lost.

Eventually, her grandpa whispered, "We need to get moving."

"But . . . but what about Grandma?" Kaelyn hiccupped, raising her head to meet his gaze.

His face was tightened with pain, but his voice remained steady. "We'll take her to the lodge. Bury her there. She always loved the North Fork."

Kaelyn nodded numbly, fresh tears spilling down her cheeks. Grandpa Terry gently disentangled himself from the front seat, leaning Joyce against the seatback. "Why don't you stay with her? Von's got a flat tire we need to fix, and then we need to make sure nothing's wrong with my truck."

As the others began to move, checking vehicles for damage and discussing their next steps, she readjusted to sit next to her grandmother on the seat. Did her grandma know? When they'd said goodbye at the church, did she know it was truly goodbye and the next time they'd see each other would be in heaven?

Von's gruff voice cut through her fog of grief. "Terry, you're bleeding."

Kaelyn's head jerked up, and her gaze landed on her grandfather. A dark stain was spreading across his right sleeve, and his face was pale from more than shock and grief.

"It's a graze," her grandpa said, but his voice was weak, and he swayed slightly on his feet.

"Let me look at that," Daisy said, stepping forward. "It's not too deep, but it needs to be cleaned and bandaged. Let's take care of it before we move on."

"Be quick about it. Von's tire needs changed, and someone needs to stand watch."

"I can stand watch," Chloe assured them.

Von nodded. "I'll take care of the tire. I'm truly sorry about Joyce."

Grandpa Terry's eyes filled with tears, and Kaelyn's own emotions spilled over.

As Daisy tended to his wound, Kaelyn leaned against her grandma, ignoring the sticky warmth of blood caressing her hand.

"I'm so sorry, Grandma," she whispered, her voice choked with tears. "I'm sorry we couldn't protect you. I'm sorry I won't get to say goodbye properly." She paused, struggling to find words. "I promise I'll take care of Grandpa. I promise I'll be strong, like you always taught me to be."

A gentle hand on her shoulder startled her. It was Daisy, her eyes red-rimmed but filled with compassion. "We need to go," she said softly. "It's not safe to stay here too long." She motioned toward Kaelyn's cheek. "I want to clean that cut first."

Kaelyn gave a halfhearted nod as Daisy put on vinyl gloves and brought an antiseptic out of her first aid kit.

"Is the tire changed?" Kaelyn asked. "Is this truck okay?" She'd noticed the hood being lifted but didn't know what had been done. Had she fallen asleep? She was still holding her grandma's hand.

"Everything is fine. This may sting," Daisy cautioned before dabbing at the cut on Kaelyn's cheek.

She winced but didn't pull away.

"It's not deep. Probably won't even leave much of a scar," Daisy assured her, smoothing the bandage into place.

Kaelyn pressed a final kiss to her grandmother's forehead before allowing Daisy to help her out of the truck.

"Maybe I should ride with Grandpa? If he's injured— "

"He wants you to ride with Chloe. He said he's fine to drive."

Kaelyn hesitated before walking over to her grandfather. He was leaning against the driver's side door, his face drawn with grief and pain.

"Grandpa," she said softly, reaching out to touch his arm. "Are you sure you're okay to drive?"

He mustered a faint smile. "I'll be fine, sweetheart. Your grandma . . . she'd want us to keep moving, to get you to safety. That's what mattered most to her. Making sure you were safe."

"I don't want to leave you alone."

"I'll be okay," he said, his voice breaking slightly. "God is by my side. He'll carry me through this. He'll be with you too. Helping you."

Kaelyn nodded, swallowing hard. She threw her arms around her grandfather, hugging him tightly. "I love you, Grandpa."

"I love you, too, honey." His embrace was fierce despite his injury. "Now go on. We need to get moving."

As they climbed back into their vehicles, the reality of their situation began to sink in. They were refugees now, fleeing from a world gone mad. The safety of Cody, of home, was behind them. Ahead lay only uncertainty and danger. Things she'd be facing without her grandma's help. Without her grandma's guidance.

Kaelyn settled into the passenger seat of the truck, Grandma Joyce's absence a physical ache in her chest. As they pulled out of the parking lot, following Von's lead once more, she turned around to look at her grandpa. His face was set in steely determination, but she could see the devastation in his eyes.

The convoy wove its way past Buffalo Bill Reservoir and the state park, where there were still several tents and camp trailers set up. Kaelyn's thoughts churned with unanswered questions. *Will we be safe at the lodge? How long will we have to stay there? Will my parents be okay in Africa? Will I ever see them again? How can I ever get by without Grandma?*

The thought of facing this new, dangerous world without Grandma Joyce's wisdom and comfort felt overwhelming. Kaelyn's chest tightened as she realized there would be no more late-night talks, no more shared laughter over inside jokes, no more gentle guidance through life's challenges.

As the miles passed, Kaelyn found herself clinging to her grandfather's words. They would bury Grandma Joyce at the lodge, in the North Fork she had loved so much. It wasn't the farewell any of them had imagined, but it was something to hold on to, a small act of normalcy in a world that had lost all sense.

The road stretched out before them, winding through the rugged landscape. Kaelyn stared out the window, watching the familiar scenery of her childhood pass by. But now, every tree and rock seemed tinged with danger, every shadow a potential threat. The North Fork of the Shoshone River meandered alongside the highway, its rushing waters a constant companion to their journey. Normally, the sight would have been comforting, but today it only served as a reminder of how quickly life could change course, sweeping away everything familiar in its path.

They were leaving behind all they had ever known and venturing into an uncertain future. The world had changed in ways they were only beginning to understand, and the journey ahead would test them in ways they couldn't imagine. Is this how Jacob felt when leaving his land for the unknown? It was different for him. He left full of hope, knowing he would soon be reunited with his long-lost son. He wasn't grieving the death of a loved one.

Kaelyn sent up a silent prayer. For strength, for protection, for some glimmer of hope in the darkness that had engulfed them.

Chloe's voice, soft and hesitant, broke the silence. "I'm so sorry about your grandma. She was a wonderful woman."

Kaelyn nodded, unable to speak past the lump in her throat.

Chloe continued, her own voice thick with emotion, "She always had a kind word for everyone. When my husband . . . when I lost him, she was there without hesitation, comforting me. All of you did. She was truly wonderful."

The sincerity in Chloe's words brought fresh tears to Kaelyn's eyes. "Thank you," she managed to whisper. "She loved helping people. She especially loved sharing about God's love. It's what made her the happiest."

As they approached the small community of Wapiti, Kaelyn tensed. The normally quiet valley seemed eerily still, save for a few people milling about outside a restaurant. Chloe slowed the truck slightly.

"Stay alert," she murmured to Kaelyn. "Just in case."

They crawled past the handful of buildings making up Wapiti's center, Kaelyn's heart pounding as she noticed a group of men eyeing their convoy suspiciously. One man stepped toward the road, but another held him back, shaking his head.

"That was tense," Chloe said, her voice shaky. "I didn't expect to see anyone out. Thought it'd be as quiet as Cody was."

Kaelyn nodded, unable to shake the feeling of unease settling over her. The encounter, brief as it was, served as a stark reminder of how quickly things had changed. People they might have waved to days ago now regarded them with suspicion and potential hostility. At least there wasn't any shooting this time. Tears once again filled her eyes.

As they pressed on, the minutes seemed to lengthen into hours. Kaelyn found herself constantly checking her phone, surprised to find only fifteen minutes had passed since Wapiti. The weight of their loss and the uncertainty ahead made time seem to crawl.

As they drove, the landscape of the North Fork unfolded around them. Towering cliffs rose on either side of the highway, their rugged faces etched with the history of millennia. Ponderosa pines clung to the rocky slopes, their dark green needles a stark contrast to the reddish-brown rock. The river, a constant presence to their right, tumbled over boulders and through rapids, its clear waters reflecting the blue sky above.

In other circumstances, Kaelyn would have marveled at the beauty surrounding them. Now she found herself scanning the cliffs and forests for potential threats, her heart racing each time a shadow moved or a bird took flight.

"Your grandma told me this was her favorite place in the world," Chloe said, her eyes fixed on the road ahead. "She told me how much she loved the North Fork of the Shoshone, that it was even more beautiful than Yellowstone Park. She said there was something about the wildness here that made her feel closer to God."

Kaelyn nodded, a small smile tugging at her lips despite her grief. "She used to say that a lot. Every time we'd go for a drive to see the wildlife or go up to hike or snowshoe, or to ski . . ." Her voice trailed off as she spotted something ahead.

As they neared Sleeping Giant Ski Lodge, a roadblock came into view. Several vehicles were parked across the highway, and armed figures stood guard.

"What do we do?" Kaelyn whispered, fear creeping into her voice. She turned to look behind them, seeing her grandfather's truck close. She reached for the walkie-talkie, her fingers brushing it as it went off.

"We have to stop," Daisy said. "Keep distance between us, and be ready to get out of here if things go bad."

Chloe swallowed hard, her eyes darting between the road ahead and the rearview mirror. "I don't like the look of this."

They followed Daisy's instructions, staying well back as the Weddles' truck came to a stop. As they approached the roadblock, Kaelyn's heart pounded. She couldn't help but think of the earlier ambush that killed her grandmother.

She glanced at her revolver and shook her head. She hadn't even reloaded. She'd been so distraught over Grandma Joyce's death, it didn't even occur to her. How many bullets did she have?

Letting out a breath, she quickly fished cartridges from her pocket, her fingers shaking as she put them in the cylinder. Whatever happened next, she knew their journey was far from over, and the challenges ahead would test them all in ways they couldn't yet imagine.

Chapter 13

Kaelyn held her breath as she watched a man from the roadblock walk toward Daisy's truck. Her heart raced, and a wave of nausea hit her. She looked over at Chloe, who was gripping the steering wheel so hard her knuckles were white.

Kaelyn's hands shook as she held the gun in her lap. She wanted to say something to Chloe but couldn't think of anything. Instead, she sat there, counting in her head to try and remain calm.

Chloe kept looking between the mirror and the guy talking to Daisy. Her jaw was tight, and Kaelyn could see sweat on her face, even though it wasn't hot in the truck.

The wait seemed endless. Kaelyn couldn't stop thinking about all the bad things that could happen. What if these guys didn't let them through? What if they tried to steal their stuff? Or something even worse?

She gripped the handgun tighter, hating she even had to think about using it. She'd shot at the men who attacked them, the ones who killed her grandma, but she was almost certain she hadn't hit anyone. Part of her wished she had. If her bullet had been true, maybe her grandma would still be alive. Maybe she could've stopped the man who killed her.

Finally, the man at the roadblock walked away from the Weddles' truck and waved at them to go through. Kaelyn let out a big breath, her shoulders dropping as the fear began to ease.

Von's voice crackled over the radio. "Everything's okay. They're part of Dick's group. He told them to expect us."

As they slowly drove past the roadblock, Kaelyn noticed the men removing their hats, their faces solemn. A fresh wave of grief washed over her as she realized they must have been told about Grandma Joyce and were paying their respects. Tears sprang to her eyes, blurring her vision as they continued their journey to the lodge.

The remaining couple of miles of the drive passed in a haze of sorrow for Kaelyn, the men's respectful gesture bringing back all the hurt. The beautiful landscape she had admired countless times before now seemed muted, as if the world itself was mourning alongside her. As they pulled up to the lodge, Kaelyn experienced both relief and apprehension.

Dick Reynolds emerged from the large house, his weathered face creased with concern. He was followed by Brian, his son who was around the same age as Kaelyn's parents. She knew him from church too. She'd also met his children when they'd been up for a visit and came to church with the family. She glanced around looking for them—a girl just younger than her and a younger boy. There were others standing on the porch, mainly women and children, but at first glance, she didn't recognize anyone.

"Should we get out?" Chloe muttered, glancing in her rearview mirror. "Your grandpa's getting out." She nodded and opened her door.

A wave of exhaustion washed over Kaelyn as she moved the revolver to the seat beside her. Her uninjured arm felt as heavy as the one with the cast as she reached for the door handle. "Just move," she whispered to herself.

Grandpa Terry came to her door. Reaching for her hand, he helped her out. "I'm here, kiddo."

Once again, Kaelyn dissolved into tears as she collapsed against him, unable to hold herself together. Her grandpa's arms wrapped around her, and she clung to him, feeling the weight of everything crashing down. It was all too much, but at least he was there.

"How's your arm? Are you okay?"

With tears filling his eyes, he gave her a nod. "Hurts some, but it'll be fine."

Dick spoke quietly with Von and Daisy before making his way to Kaelyn and her grandpa. "I'm so sorry for your loss," he said, his voice gentle. "Joyce was a wonderful woman. She'll be deeply missed."

Kaelyn nodded, unable to form words past the lump in her throat. She tried to stand tall, to be strong like she imagined her grandmother would have wanted, but inside, she was crumbling. She was grateful for her grandpa's arm around her shoulders.

Ruth Reynolds, Dick's wife, cleared her throat, catching Kaelyn's attention. She stood there, looking determined and all business. "Come on, girl. Let's get you inside. Grab what you need for now. We'll worry about unloading things in a bit."

Kaelyn allowed herself to be led away, casting a glance back at her grandfather's truck where Brian was helping to remove Grandma Joyce's body. Fresh tears spilled down her cheeks as Ruth guided her into the lodge.

The interior of the spacious lodge was warm and rustic, but Kaelyn barely noticed. She felt small and lost, overwhelmed by grief and uncertainty. Ruth's brisk manner, so different from her grandmother's warmth, only heightened her feelings of insecurity.

"You'll be sharing a room with the woman you arrived with," Ruth informed her, leading her down a hallway. "Bathroom's at the end of the hall. Kitchen's off-limits unless you're on duty in there. Everyone works together here. You don't work, you don't eat. Just like the Good Book says."

Kaelyn nodded, unable to speak. She wanted to thank Ruth and ask questions, to do something other than stand there feeling useless, but the words wouldn't come. Her grandmother would have known what to say, how to handle this. But Grandma Joyce was gone, and Kaelyn was lost without her.

As they reached the room, Ruth paused, her expression softening slightly. "I know this is hard," she said, her tone still businesslike but with a hint of kindness. "But we all have to pull our weight here. Take some time to settle in, then come help with the unloading."

Kaelyn managed a weak "okay" as Ruth left her at the door. She entered the room, noting the two single beds and sparse furnishings. Sinking onto one of the beds, she finally allowed herself to break down, her body shaking with quiet sobs.

She wasn't sure how long she sat there, lost in her grief, before a knock at the door jolted her back to the present. Grandpa Terry entered, looking as sad as she felt.

"We'll bury her later today or tomorrow morning," he said, his voice rough. "They'll use the tractor to dig the grave as best they can. We chose a spot up on the hill."

Kaelyn wiped her eyes. "Okay, Grandpa."

As he turned to leave, Ruth appeared in the doorway. "I heard you were injured, Terry. Let me take a look at it."

He waved her off. "It's fine. Daisy bandaged it up. I want to get the trucks unloaded."

Ruth's lips thinned, but she didn't argue. As they left, Kaelyn knew she should follow, should help with the unloading. But the thought of facing everyone, of trying to be useful when she was so lost and broken, was almost paralyzing.

She took a deep breath, trying to summon the strength. Grandma Joyce wouldn't want her to hide away, no matter how tempting it was. With shaky legs, Kaelyn stood and made her way to the door. She paused, her hand on the doorknob, fighting the urge to stay in the safety of the room.

"You can do this," she whispered to herself. "You have to do this."

With one more deep breath, Kaelyn opened the door and stepped out into the hallway. The lodge buzzed with activity as people moved back and forth, carrying supplies and organizing. She shrank back, out of place and unsure where to start or how to help.

Chloe appeared at her side, her eyes red-rimmed but her voice steady. "Come on," she said gently. "Let's go see what needs to be done."

Grateful for the guidance, Kaelyn followed Chloe outside. The afternoon sun was bright, all suggestions of earlier rain clouds gone, a stark contrast to the darkness she felt inside. She squinted, taking in the scene before her. Their small convoy of vehicles was parked near the main lodge, and people were efficiently unloading supplies and gear.

Grandpa Terry was there, stubbornly lifting boxes despite his injury. Kaelyn wanted to tell him to rest, to let others handle it, but she knew he needed this. Needed to keep moving, to feel useful in the face of overwhelming loss.

Dick approached them, wiping his brow with a bandanna. "Chloe, we could use a hand organizing the food supplies in the kitchen. Kaelyn, why don't you help sort through the personal belongings? Make sure everyone's stuff gets to the right places. We're putting your grandpa in the small room off the kitchen. Von and Daisy have the cabin over there." He pointed toward a string of six cabins. "The one on the far end. They'll be sharing with two other couples."

Kaelyn nodded, grateful for the clear direction. As she moved toward the trucks, she couldn't help but notice the sidelong glances and whispers from the others. She knew they meant well and their sympathy was genuine, but it made her feel exposed, vulnerable.

She began moving bags and boxes, trying to focus on that rather than the crushing weight of her grief. As she worked, she overheard snippets of conversation . . . worried discussions about food supplies, security measures, and how long they might need to stay at the lodge.

In addition to Dick and Ruth Reynolds, who had a room in the main lodge, their son Brian also lived on-site, staying in one of the larger cabins. And there were at least a dozen others there. One lady caught her gaze and gave a sad smile. She looked familiar but Kaelyn couldn't place her.

Their new reality started to sink in. This wasn't simply a temporary measure. They were refugees now, fleeing a world that had become unrecognizable. And Kaelyn had no idea how to navigate the new reality without her grandmother's guidance.

As she lifted a particularly heavy bag, a wave of dizziness washed over her. She stumbled, and the bag slipped from her grasp as she lost her footing. Strong hands steadied her, and she looked up to see Brian, Dick's son.

"Whoa, easy there," he said, his voice kind. "Why don't you take a break? You've been at this for a while now."

Kaelyn shook her head, embarrassed by her weakness. "No, I'm fine. I need to keep helping." A vision of Ruth's stern demeanor flashed in her mind, and she knew she couldn't let herself fall apart. Taking a deep breath, she wiped her eyes and tried to steady herself.

Brian's expression was understanding but firm. "You need to rest. I'm sure your grandfather will agree with me. Come on, I'll walk you back to the lodge."

As they walked, the fatigue of the day—both physical and emotional—settled into Kaelyn's bones. Brian's presence was comforting in its steadiness, reminding her of the way her father would guide her after a long day of hiking.

"I'm sorry about your grandmother," Brian said as they reached the lodge's porch. "She was an amazing woman. Always so kind to everyone."

Tears pricked at her eyes again. "She was. I don't know how to do this without her."

Brian was quiet for a moment. "None of us know how to do this. We're all figuring it out as we go. Things are more different now than they've ever been." He shifted his gaze off in the distance. "None of us know what tomorrow will bring. But you're here and you're safe. I'm sure that is what your grandmother wanted."

His words, simple as they were, provided a small measure of comfort. Kaelyn managed a weak smile. "Thank you."

As Brian headed back to help with the unloading, Kaelyn sank into one of the porch chairs. She watched the activity in the yard, feeling simultaneously part of the group and apart from it. The grief was still there, a constant ache in her chest, but alongside it was a tiny spark of something else. Perhaps not hope, not yet, but the beginnings of resilience.

She thought of her parents. Were they safe? She needed to grab her laptop, check if there was internet, and send them a message about Grandma Joyce. Her mom had lost both her parents a few years ago and would now be helping her dad cope with the grief of losing his mom. She wished they were here, with her and Grandpa Terry, to share in the mourning.

Kaelyn saw her grandfather approaching. He looked tired, the bandage on his arm a stark reminder of their harrowing journey. But there was a determination in his stride, a strength she envied.

He sat down beside her, groaning softly as he eased into the chair. For a long moment, they sat in silence, watching as the last of the supplies were unloaded and people began to drift toward the lodge.

"Your grandmother . . ." Grandpa Terry began, his voice rough with emotion. "She always said you were stronger than you knew. Braver than you believed."

Kaelyn turned to look at him, seeing the grief etched deep in the lines of his face. "I don't feel strong or brave right now, Grandpa," she admitted.

He reached out, taking her hand in his. His palm was calloused and warm, a familiar comfort. "Strength isn't about not feeling scared or sad, sweetheart. It's about feeling those things and moving forward anyway. That's what you're doing right now."

Kaelyn felt tears welling up again, but they weren't entirely tears of sorrow. There was gratitude there, too, and love for her grandfather, who always seemed to say the right thing.

"We're going to get through this." He squeezed her hand. "It won't be easy, and there will be days when it feels impossible. But we'll do it together. For your grandma. For your parents. For each other."

"Did they finish digging the . . ." Kaelyn cleared her throat and shook her head.

"Dick went to check. He thinks they did all they could with the tractor and they're using shovels now. He said he thought it'd be tomorrow, after all. Both Dick and Brian have guard duty at one of the roadblocks in a short while."

Kaelyn's stomach let out a loud rumble. She placed her hand over it, as her grandpa shook his head. "Sorry, kiddo. It's been such a day. Let's find you something to eat."

"I have snacks in my backpack. Grandma told me— " Her voice caught as the tears returned. In a quiet voice, she said, "Grandma said things may be crazy today and I should make sure I had food."

"That sounds exactly like what she told me. I have things in my pack too. Let's go over to the picnic table under the tree. Your grandma would tan my hide if I didn't make sure to keep you healthy."

He gave her a watery smile and reached for her hand. Kaelyn knew deep in her soul that Grandpa Terry would do all he could to take care of her, exactly as her grandma would want. For now, until her parents came home, it was the two of them.

Chapter 14

Kaelyn stood at her grandma's grave, staring at the wooden cross. Grandma Joyce died on Thursday, and they buried her early Friday morning. Now it was Sunday, and Kaelyn had come here every day since, usually several times a day.

There wasn't a real headstone but rather the rustic cross Grandpa Terry had made. He was at the grave with her, like he had been most times. Yesterday, he'd sung a song about an old wooden cross. He messed up some of the words, but Kaelyn remembered him saying Grandma Joyce had already traded her cross for a crown in heaven.

"Ready to head back?" her grandpa asked, his voice rough.

Kaelyn took one last look at the cross before turning away. As they walked down the hill toward the lodge, she noticed Grandpa was breathing hard and sweating.

"You okay?" she asked, concern tightening her chest.

He waved her off. "I'm fine, just hot." He took off his baseball cap and wiped his forehead with a hankie.

She wasn't sure she believed him but didn't push it. As they neared the bottom of the slope, her foot caught on a loose rock. She stumbled, her arms flailing before she managed to catch herself against the side of a large bush.

"Careful," he said, looking over his shoulder with a raised eyebrow.

Kaelyn straightened up quickly, pretending she wasn't a second away from face-planting into the dirt. "I'm fine," she muttered, brushing her hands off.

When they got back to the lodge, Kaelyn said, "I need to go help in the kitchen." She didn't want to, but she knew she had to do her part.

"All right, sweetheart. I'll see you later."

Kaelyn watched him go, still worried. She knew he, Von, Daisy, and Chloe all had to do guard duty and other jobs around the lodge. Because of her broken arm, Kaelyn couldn't do guard duty, but she tried to help out where she could. She didn't think her grandpa should be taking guard duty either, not after being shot, but he seemed to be healing well enough and insisted on doing his part.

In the kitchen, Ruth was organizing lunch prep. "There you are," she said when Kaelyn walked in. "Can you wash those vegetables?"

Kaelyn nodded and got to work. It wasn't easy with her cast, but she managed. As she washed carrots, her mind drifted to her parents. She'd tried to reach them so many times. The Reynolds had the new low-orbit satellite internet system that seemed to work, and her emails showed as sent, but there were no replies. She'd tried calling and texting, too, but the phone never rang and the texts, while seeming to go through, got no response.

Were her parents okay? Was it some problem with electronics, or something worse? Kaelyn tried to push the worry away. She had to trust they were all right. That's what her grandmother would do.

Grandma Joyce always seemed to know what to say. She'd probably tell Kaelyn today's troubles were enough for today and remind her that God was in control. Kaelyn wanted to be like Grandma Joyce. Strong and sure, knowing what to do.

Even Chloe, who was pregnant and had recently lost her husband, seemed to be holding it together. *If Chloe can do it*, Kaelyn told herself, *so can I.*

"Earth to Kaelyn," Ruth's voice broke into her thoughts. "Those carrots clean yet?"

"Oh, sorry," she said, realizing she'd been scrubbing the same carrot for way too long. "Almost done."

Ruth softened a bit. "I know you've got a lot on your mind. Try to focus on the task at hand, all right?"

Kaelyn nodded, determined to do better. She finished the carrots and moved on to the potatoes, trying to keep her mind on the work.

Later, as they were serving lunch, Kaelyn noticed her grandpa wasn't there. "Has anyone seen Grandpa Terry?" she asked Chloe, who was helping dish out food.

Chloe shook her head. "Not since this morning. Maybe he's on guard duty?"

Kaelyn frowned. She was pretty sure he wasn't supposed to be on duty until later. "I'm going to go check on him," she said, putting down her serving spoon.

"Kaelyn," Ruth called after her, "we're not done here."

"I know, I'll be right back. I need to make sure he's okay."

She hurried out of the dining room and to the room her grandpa was staying in. Knocking on the door, she called out, "Grandpa? You in there?"

There was no answer. She tried the handle and found it unlocked. She pushed the door open slowly. "Grandpa?"

He was there, lying on the bed. For a second, Kaelyn's heart stopped, thinking the worst. But then she saw his chest rise and fall. He was sleeping.

Relief washed over her, but it was quickly replaced by worry again. It wasn't like him to miss lunch or to sleep in the middle of the day.

She walked over to the bed and gently shook his shoulder. "Grandpa? You okay?"

He stirred, blinking up at her. "Kaelyn? What time is it?"

"It's lunchtime. You weren't there, so I came to check on you."

He sat up slowly, rubbing his face. "I'm sorry, kiddo. Got a little tired. Must've dozed off."

Kaelyn studied his face. He looked pale and there were dark circles under his eyes. "Are you sure you're okay? Maybe we should have Daisy take a look at you."

Grandpa Terry shook his head. "No need. I'm fine. Needed a little rest. Let's go get some lunch, okay?"

Kaelyn wasn't convinced, but she didn't want to argue. "Okay, if you're sure."

They walked to the dining room together, Kaelyn watching her grandpa closely. He seemed steady enough, but she knew something was wrong.

In the dining room, Ruth gave her a pointed look. "There you are. We could've used your help finishing up."

"Sorry," Kaelyn mumbled. "I was checking on Grandpa."

Ruth's expression softened a bit when she saw Grandpa Terry. "Everything all right? You look pale . . . and flushed at the same time."

"Just fine," he said, forcing a smile. "I'm starving."

As they sat down to eat, Kaelyn noticed Von and Dick having an intense conversation in the corner. She couldn't hear what they were saying, but their expressions were serious.

Even though her grandpa said he was starving, he picked at his food, moving it around more than eating it.

After lunch, Kaelyn helped clean up, trying to make up for leaving earlier. As she was drying dishes, Daisy came into the kitchen. "Rumor has it your grandpa was looking a little poorly at lunch."

Kaelyn gave a nod. "He was napping before lunch, and he barely ate."

"Where is he now?"

Shrugging, Kaelyn shook her head. "He said he was going to go out and check on the livestock, see if Dick or Brian needed any help. He has guard duty at the Pahaska roadblock later."

Daisy gave a wave and set off to find Grandpa Terry.

Dick and the others had set up a roadblock on both ends of the newly formed community. The east-end roadblock was the one they'd encountered right before Sleeping Giant Ski Area and the Sleepy G Guest Ranch across the road. The west end was the other side of the historic Pahaska Tepee Resort, Buffalo Bill's Original Lodge, only two miles from the East Gate of Yellowstone National Park.

Even though Yellowstone was closed, and the entrance gated, they'd still had people come through on foot. Their procedure was to escort folks through the stretch of territory the three lodges had claimed. When giving them an overview of life at the lodge, Dick had stressed the importance of the security measures they had in place and how the three lodges—Sleepy G, Pahaska Teepee, and his own place, East Gate Lodge and Cabins—were working together.

Kaelyn thought the roadblocks were a good idea but knew they weren't foolproof. There were plenty of trails off the road that allowed people to easily bypass the guards. She and her family had snowshoed and cross-country skied in the area enough for her to know her way around. Still, it was better than nothing she supposed.

The merger offered security and pooled resources. Both Sleepy G and Pahaska had trail horses, while Sleepy G also kept a small cattle herd. The Reynolds contributed a couple of dairy cows and a large flock of chickens. Most of the seasonal staff, many of whom had lived on-site, had left early on when the resorts shut down. Those who stayed either couldn't fly home with the airports closed or were year-round employees who lived at the resorts.

The Reynolds had two people they hired to help at their place, both had left for home as soon as they were given the opportunity. The people currently living at East Gate Lodge and Cabins were specially invited by the family. Many, like Kaelyn and her grandpa, were friends from church. Others were people they knew before purchasing the lodge a few years prior, having driven from various locations in Wyoming and surrounding states.

Brian hoped his ex-wife and children, who lived in Casper, would come up to the lodge. Casper, along with Cheyenne, Gillette, Sheridan, and Evanston all had travel restrictions, with the Wyoming National Guard in place. While Kaelyn could understand limiting travel so the Star Bright sickness didn't spread, she wasn't clear as to how the towns were chosen to have these restrictions.

Cheyenne and Evanston made sense, with them both being near state lines and on Interstate 80. Sheridan, too, for that matter, with it being the nearest large town on I-90 after entering Wyoming from Montana.

But Gillette was around ninety miles from the South Dakota state line. Yes, it was on I-90, which had been heavily traveled before the disaster started, but why have a military presence there? Maybe they had guards at the state line, too, and Kaelyn hadn't heard about it?

Casper having travel restrictions made little sense. It was smack dab in the middle of the state. Grandpa Terry said he suspected it was because of the size of the city, being the second largest—behind Cheyenne—in the state.

Because of the travel restrictions, Brian's family was not only hesitant to leave Casper but were now unable. There were rumors that the governor was going to let up on the rules and allow people to at least leave Casper. Brian had been doing his best to stay in contact with the family and had encouraged them to have things packed and ready to go.

Casper had its share of troubles and was hit hard by the Star Brights. Brian didn't share many details, but he mentioned his family had been caught up in dangerous situations and were lucky to have escaped with their lives. Kaelyn overheard him quietly telling his dad, Dick, he should have left on the first day of the explosions in Casper—the same day as the shooting at the doctor's office and the incident at the Irma—and brought his kids here sooner.

Kaelyn had met his daughter last year when she visited, and they came to church. She was younger than Kaelyn but seemed much older. She had an air of confidence about her that made Kaelyn feel small and unsure of herself. While Kaelyn often questioned her own choices, this girl carried herself with an easy self-assuredness. Being around her brought a mix of admiration and insecurity, as Kaelyn couldn't help but wish she could share that same sense of poise and purpose.

The rattle of a pan brought Kaelyn back to the task at hand. "Those dishes aren't going to put themselves away," Ruth said, shaking her head. "You spend far too much time woolgathering."

"Sorry," Kaelyn muttered. Hot tears pricked at her eyes, and she angrily wiped them away. She was tired of crying, tired of feeling helpless and scared. *Grandma wouldn't cry*, she told herself. *Grandma would pray and find a way to help.*

Taking a deep breath, she smiled. "I'll get these put away. Then what would you like me to do?"

The rest of the afternoon passed in a blur of chores and worried thoughts. Kaelyn helped fold laundry, tidied up the common areas, and even assisted another woman with feeding the chickens and gathering eggs. She also spent some time playing fetch with the Reynolds's dog. Her grandpa had left for his shift at the roadblock. She noted he seemed to look a little better, not as tired and with a little more color. Daisy had checked his wound and rebandaged it. She said it didn't look bad, but not great either. She'd check it again in the morning.

As evening approached, Kaelyn sat on the front porch, watching the sun sink behind the mountains. The view was beautiful, but she couldn't shake the heaviness in her heart.

Chloe came out and sat beside her. For a while, they sat in silence, looking out at the fading light.

Finally, Chloe spoke. "It's okay, you know. To not be okay."

Kaelyn glanced at her, surprised. "What do you mean?"

Chloe sighed. "I mean, it's okay to be sad, to be scared. You don't have to be strong all the time."

Her throat tightened. "But you seem to be managing it all so well. And Grandma, she was always so strong."

"Trust me," Chloe said, "I'm a mess most of the time. I hide it. And I bet your grandma had her moments too. Being strong doesn't mean never feeling things. It means you feel those things and keep going anyway."

Kaelyn felt tears coming again, but this time she didn't try to stop them. "I miss her so much," she whispered. "And I'm so worried about Grandpa, my parents, and my friends still in Cody. I'm even worried about people I don't know, wondering how we're ever going to get through this. I don't know what to do."

Chloe put her arm around Kaelyn. "You're doing it. You're here, you're helping, you're surviving. That's all any of us can do right now."

They sat there as it got dark, and Kaelyn let herself cry. For the first time in days, she thought maybe it was okay to not have all the answers, to not be perfectly strong all the time.

As they got up to go inside, Kaelyn turned to Chloe. "Thanks," she said. "For everything."

Chloe smiled, and it reached her eyes. "Anytime."

Kaelyn felt a little better as they went back into the lodge. She didn't know what was going to happen tomorrow, but for now, knowing she wasn't alone was enough.

That night, lying in bed, her mind wandered through it all. About her grandma and the wooden cross on the hill. About her grandpa and how she needed to keep a closer eye on him. And about her parents. She said a quick prayer for them to be safe.

As she was falling asleep, Kaelyn thought about what Chloe said. Maybe being strong didn't mean never being scared. Maybe it meant facing each day as it came, doing what needed to be done, and letting yourself feel what you felt.

It wasn't much, but it was a start. And for now, it would have to be enough.

Chapter 15

Kaelyn woke early, determined to face the day with the strength her grandmother would have wanted. She dressed quickly and pulled her hair into a high ponytail before heading to the kitchen, ready to help with breakfast preparations.

As she went down the stairs, she thought about Jacob from the Bible. God had led him to Egypt and given him and his family a good life there. Had God led the Fishers to the lodge? She wanted to believe He had, but losing Grandma Joyce filled her with doubt.

The lodge was already bustling with activity when she entered the kitchen. Ruth was directing a small group of helpers, assigning tasks with her usual efficiency. The smell of coffee and frying bacon filled the air, a deceptively normal scent in a world that had changed so drastically. Kaelyn tried to focus on these familiar routines, pushing away thoughts of her parents far away in Africa and the uncertainty seeming to loom over everything now.

Seeing Kaelyn, Ruth lifted her chin to summon her. "You're late. I expected you here at five thirty."

"Um . . . sorry." She had glanced at her phone when leaving her room. She was late, but only by two or three minutes.

"We had some new folks show up last night. Friends of Brian's. They came down from Billings." Ruth put her hands on her hips. "He said there are now roadblocks set up in Cody."

"Roadblocks? The National Guard?"

"Some, yes. But also regular folks. Patriots. They set them up after the trouble you had passing through. He heard the shooters were . . . eliminated."

Tears filled Kaelyn's eyes. "Grandma's killers?"

Ruth lifted her shoulder. "I assume so. Now, let's get on with fixing breakfast."

"Wait," Kaelyn said, her curiosity overcoming her usual shyness. "What else did they say about Cody?"

Ruth sighed, clearly impatient to get back to work. "The new folks said it's pretty rough there. Power's spotty at best. The hospital's overwhelmed. Not only Cody, but Billings was terrible too. Even with the rations and food drops, supplies are getting scarce in some areas."

"What about the roadblocks?" Kaelyn pressed.

"They heard there were checkpoints on every highway into town. They were stopped on Highway 120, coming down from Billings. There's also one on the Powell-Cody Highway, the Greybull Highway, and the road to Meeteetse, plus a barricade near the Stampede grounds. They're checking everyone coming and going. Apparently, there was trouble with looters from out of town."

Kaelyn's mind reeled. It was hard to imagine her hometown turned into a fortress. "Are people still . . . you know, getting sick?"

Ruth's face softened. "Some. But not as many as before. They think the worst of it might be over, at least in Cody. Maybe the virus has burned itself out? Now, unless you have any more questions, those pancakes won't mix themselves."

As Kaelyn turned to her task, she overheard Ruth muttering to another helper about the long journey the newcomers had made from Billings, dodging roadblocks and unfriendly groups along the way. It sounded like things weren't any better in Montana.

While mixing the pancake batter, Kaelyn's mind kept circling back to what Ruth had said about the shooters being "eliminated." She should've felt something about that news. Relief? Satisfaction? But all she felt was a hollow emptiness. The men who killed her grandmother were gone, but so was Grandma Joyce. Nothing could bring her back.

Part of her was glad they couldn't hurt anyone else. But another part, a part that scared her a little, wished she could've seen them face consequences. Real consequences, not just . . . elimination.

What did that even mean in this new world? Executed? Killed in a shootout? The old Kaelyn would have been horrified at the thought of anyone dying, even bad people. But now? Doubt clouded her mind, and a sense of uncertainty gnawed at her.

Would Grandma have wanted this? she wondered, her movements slowing as she stirred. Grandma Joyce had always preached forgiveness, even for the worst offenses. But she'd also believed in justice. In this strange new reality, where courtrooms and prisons seemed like relics of a lost world, maybe this was what justice looked like now.

The realization left her feeling uneasy. If this was the new normal, she wasn't sure she was ready for it.

Continuing with breakfast preparations, Kaelyn kept glancing at the closed door of her grandfather's room. Breakfast came and went, but Grandpa Terry didn't appear.

"Don't worry," Daisy said, noticing Kaelyn's concerned looks. "I checked on him last night. His wound needed some attention, so I told him to rest up today. He's following orders." She gave a smile and patted Kaelyn on the arm.

Despite Daisy's reassurances, Kaelyn couldn't shake the feeling something was wrong. She'd always been prone to worry, a trait her grandmother had gently tried to help her overcome. "Worry is like a rocking chair," Grandma Joyce would say. "It gives you something to do, but it doesn't get you anywhere." Kaelyn smiled at the memory, then felt a pang of grief. She missed her grandmother's wisdom now more than ever.

Kaelyn threw herself into the morning chores, scrubbing floors and folding laundry with fierce determination. Doing the work one handed wasn't easy, but she was developing suitable workarounds. As the morning wore on and her grandpa still didn't emerge, her unease grew.

By midmorning, Kaelyn couldn't stand it anymore. She approached the small room off the kitchen where Grandpa Terry was staying. Originally used as the cook's room by the previous owners, it wasn't much, but he'd said he liked the view of the backyard and garden. "Your grandma would have loved it," he'd told her more than once, his voice wistful.

Kaelyn knocked softly. "Grandpa? You awake?" No answer. She knocked again, louder this time. Still nothing.

"Grandpa, I'm coming in, okay?" she called out as she turned the doorknob.

The room was dim, curtains drawn against the morning light. As her eyes adjusted, Kaelyn's heart clenched. He lay motionless on the bed, his face pale and drawn.

She rushed to his side. "Grandpa?" Her voice came out small and scared, nothing like the brave front she'd been trying to put on.

His breathing was labored, each inhale a struggle. Heat radiated from his skin when she touched his forehead. "Grandpa, wake up," Kaelyn pleaded, gently shaking his shoulder. But his eyes remained closed.

Panic rose in her throat as she ran from the room. "Daisy!" she called out, her voice cracking. "Daisy, help!"

Daisy appeared from the dining room, alarm clear on her face. "What is it?"

"It's Grandpa," Kaelyn managed. "He won't wake up. He's burning up."

Daisy didn't waste a second. She hurried to his room with Kaelyn on her heels. She bent over the bed and checked his pulse.

"How long has he been like this?"

"I don't know," she said, fighting back tears. "I only found him minutes ago. Like this."

Daisy carefully examined the wound on Grandpa Terry's arm, her frown deepening. "It doesn't look terrible, but . . . this fever. I'm worried it might be a systemic infection."

"What does that mean?"

"It means we need to get him to a hospital. Stay with him. Talk to him. I'm going to make arrangements for transport."

As Daisy hurried out, Kaelyn pulled a chair close to the bed and took her grandfather's hand. It was hot and dry in hers.

"Grandpa?" she said softly. "We're going to take you to the hospital and get you fixed up." She swallowed hard, trying to keep her voice steady. "They still take emergencies. They'll know what to do."

His eyelids fluttered, and for a moment, Kaelyn's heart leaped. But then Grandpa Terry spoke, his voice barely a whisper. "No hospital."

"Grandpa, you have to go," she insisted, squeezing his hand. "You're really sick."

He shook his head slightly. "I'm sorry, Kaelyn. I don't want to leave you on your own." His words were slow and labored. "Dick and Ruth, they'll watch out for you."

"Don't talk like that. You're going to be fine. We'll get you to the doctor and— "

"Kaelyn," her grandpa interrupted, his eyes opening. "Listen to me. I love you so much. You've been such a blessing."

Tears spilled down her cheeks. "I love you, too, Grandpa. Please, just hold on. Daisy's getting help. We'll drive you back to Cody and take you to the hospital. They'll know what to do to make you well."

But Grandpa Terry's eyes had closed again. His breathing grew more labored, each inhale a rattling struggle.

Kaelyn held his hand tighter. She should go get Daisy, or Dick, or anyone. But she couldn't bear the thought of leaving him alone, even for a moment.

"Do you remember that time we drove down to Douglas for the weekend to go to the state fair?" she whispered, her throat tight. "You won that huge stuffed bear, and I couldn't believe you carried it around the whole time. And then it took up so much room in the backseat. You teased me that he was my new baby brother."

She wiped her tears. "Or when you tried to teach me to drive the stick shift you borrowed from your friend and I kept stalling out? You said everyone should know how to drive a manual. You were so patient."

She continued, desperately reaching for memories that felt like lifelines. Camping trips and holiday dinners flooded her mind; the time she won the spelling bee, pride shining in his eyes.

All the while, Grandpa Terry's breathing grew more shallow and irregular. Kaelyn's words came faster, more frantic, as if she could somehow keep him there through sheer force of will.

"Remember how you always said I was braver than I knew? I'm not brave, Grandpa. I'm scared and awkward and clumsy. I need you to stay with me. Please."

But the pauses between his breaths grew longer. Kaelyn held her grandfather's hand to her cheek, feeling the fading warmth of his skin.

"I love you," she whispered. "It's okay. Grandma's waiting for you."

With one last, quiet exhale, Grandpa Terry grew still.

She sat frozen, unable to process what happened. It didn't seem real. Any moment now, he'd open his eyes. He'd smile at her and say it was all a mistake.

The door opened, and Daisy's voice broke the silence. "Everything's set. We can take him to the hospital now."

Kaelyn looked up, her face tear-stained and pale. "There's no need," she said, her voice hollow. "He's gone to be with Grandma Joyce. With God."

Daisy's face fell. She crossed the room quickly, checking for a pulse. "Oh, Kaelyn. I'm so sorry."

But Kaelyn barely heard her. She was lost in a fog of grief, still clutching her grandfather's hand. In the span of only a few days, she'd lost both her grandparents, the two people who had been her anchors, her safe harbor in this terrifying new world.

Daisy's arm went around her shoulders as she murmured words of comfort. But it all seemed far away and unreal. All Kaelyn could focus on was the still form of her grandfather, and the crushing weight of loss threatening to overwhelm her yet again.

Chapter 16

Kaelyn stood among the small group gathered around the open grave, the freshly turned earth making everything feel so final. The wooden cross for her grandfather lay nearby, waiting to be placed once the burial was complete.

For reasons she didn't fully understand, her grandpa had made the cross himself, filling in his name and date of birth but leaving his date of death blank. It looked exactly like Grandma Joyce's marker.

Daisy said she thought he'd made them at the same time. Daisy was the one who'd found the cross in his room, shortly after he passed away.

Kaelyn blinked hard, fighting back tears. She had to be strong now. Chloe stood close on her left, a steady presence despite her own grief. On Kaelyn's right, Daisy kept a supportive hand on her shoulder.

The small gathering of lodge residents began to sing "Amazing Grace," their voices carrying on the mountain breeze. Kaelyn's throat tightened, making it hard to join in. The words were hollow and meaningless in the face of so much loss.

As the last notes faded, Dick stepped forward to lead "The Old Rugged Cross." Kaelyn had requested it, remembering how her grandpa had sung it a few days prior when they visited Grandma Joyce's grave.

She thought of her grandfather's words about her grandmother trading her cross for a crown in heaven. Now Grandpa Terry had his crown too. The image brought a fresh wave of pain. They were together now, worshipping with Jesus, but she was alone. Left in Wyoming with people she barely knew.

Alone. The word echoed in Kaelyn's mind, bringing fresh pain. She thought of her parents, so far away in Africa. She'd texted them shortly after her grandpa died. There was, as usual, no response. Last night, she'd sent them an email, pouring out her heart about everything that had happened. But there was still no reply. What if something had happened to them too? What if she was completely alone in the world now?

Kaelyn straightened her shoulders, blinking away tears. No, she couldn't think like that. She had to be strong, had to do whatever it took to survive this disaster. Her grandparents would've wanted that. Her parents would be counting on it. Soon this would be over, and they'd be able to come home, and she had to be there. She had to be the one still alive.

As Dick wrapped up the brief service, shouts rang out from one of the nearby cabins. The gathered group turned, muttering in confusion and annoyance.

"Someone needs to tell them how to behave properly," one woman said, her voice sharp with disapproval.

But Chloe grabbed Kaelyn's arm, her grip tight. "I hope it's a simple domestic dispute," she whispered, her eyes wide with concern.

The noise from the cabin grew louder, angry voices raised in an argument. Then, almost immediately, they fell silent.

Dick cleared his throat. "I'll have a talk with them about proper etiquette," he said, his tone firm. "They're new. Recently arrived. Sorry about the interruption, friends. Let's go ahead and pray."

As Dick paused to allow everyone to bow their heads, the cabin door where the shouting had occurred flew open. A teenage boy, somewhere around Kaelyn's age, stormed out, slamming the door behind him. The sound echoed across the hillside, making several people jump.

When the prayer ended, the group began to break apart. Dick gestured to one of the men, speaking in clipped tones out of earshot, and nodded toward the cabin where the shouting had come from.

Before they could head that way, a man stepped out of the cabin. Judging by his age, Kaelyn guessed he was the teen's father. With his head down and his hands buried in his pockets, he shuffled toward the horse pasture. Dick and the other man followed him.

Chloe wrapped her arm around Kaelyn's shoulder. Soon, it was only the two of them. "I'm here for you," she said softly. "Whatever you need."

Kaelyn nodded, grateful for Chloe's kindness. They stood in silence for a moment, gazing at the beautiful landscape that now seemed alien and lonely. Her grandma had loved the North Fork, and now she and Grandpa Terry would reside there forever.

"They loved you, you know." Chloe tightened her arm around Kaelyn. "I spoke with your grandma one day, before this whole Star Bright mess started. It was a day or so after you fell and broke your arm. She told me about how you were planning to go to Africa with your parents but wouldn't be able to. She was sad for you, missing out on something you'd been so looking forward to, but also excited to have time with you. She told me what an amazing person you are. She was right, Kaelyn. You're amazing and stronger than you know. You're going to be okay."

"I don't know." Kaelyn shook her head. "I don't feel like I'm going to be okay."

Chloe sighed. "I know. It's the same for me."

"I–I'm sorry."

A scream ripped through the air, followed by several gunshots. Both women spun toward the cabins. More shouts followed, mingling with fear and confusion.

"What's happening?" Kaelyn asked, her voice shaking.

Before Chloe could answer, movement caught Kaelyn's eye. The teenage boy was walking toward them, his gait unsteady. As he drew closer, Kaelyn clutched Chloe's arm. The boy was covered in blood, and a knife was in his right hand. And he was humming.

"Chloe," Kaelyn whispered, fear closing her throat. "He's a Star Bright."

They were unarmed, their weapons left behind out of respect for the funeral. It was the two of them against the blood-covered boy.

Chloe pushed Kaelyn behind her, backing away slowly. "We need to run," she said, her voice low and urgent.

But it was too late. The boy's eyes locked on to them, and a twisted smile spread across his face as the humming morphed into singing. The melody was unfamiliar to Kaelyn, but the word "star" echoed in what must have been the chorus.

Kaelyn's heart pounded, but her body didn't seem to catch up. As they turned to flee, her foot caught on a tree root half-hidden in the dirt. She pitched forward, her arms flailing as she tried to catch herself.

"Kaelyn!" Chloe shouted, her voice sharp.

Kaelyn hit the ground hard, the impact jarring her bones, but she scrambled to push herself up, her breath catching in her throat. The boy's singing echoed behind them, cold and merciless.

"Go!" Chloe yelled, grabbing Kaelyn's arm and hauling her to her feet. But the damage was done. Every second they lost now made their escape that much harder.

The boy's gaze fixed on them as he fell silent. He lunged forward, knife raised.

Chloe shoved Kaelyn hard, sending her stumbling to the side as the knife slashed through the air where she'd been standing. Chloe dodged the other way, trying to draw the boy's attention.

"Run, Kaelyn!" Chloe shouted.

But Kaelyn couldn't leave her pregnant friend. She scrambled to her feet, looking for anything she could use as a weapon. Her eyes fell on a heavy branch fallen from a nearby tree.

The boy turned toward Chloe, his humming growing louder. Kaelyn seized her chance and darted forward to grab the branch. It was awkward with her broken arm, but adrenaline gave her strength.

"Hey!" Kaelyn yelled, swinging the branch with all her might.

It connected with the boy's shoulder, throwing him off balance. He whirled toward her, eyes wild, the humming once again returning. "That's not what The One wants," he said in a sing-song voice.

Kaelyn backpedaled, the branch held in front of her, poking it to keep him at bay. His humming grew louder.

Chloe took advantage of the distraction and tackled the boy from behind. They went down in a tangle of limbs, the knife flying from his hand.

Kaelyn's heart pounded as she watched them struggle. Chloe was fighting hard, but the boy was bigger and stronger. He managed to flip them over, pinning Chloe beneath him.

On the ground, Chloe squirmed, but he held her with little effort. The singing returned.

"Number the stars, one by one, mark the moments 'til the dawn. Even when the night feels far too long, we'll number the stars, and carry on."

"Get off me, you freak!" Chloe shouted, twisting her body as she drove her knee upward, catching him off guard and making him lose his grip.

Kaelyn took advantage of the way the boy went off balance and charged forward. She brought her cast down hard on the back of his head. He reeled, momentarily stunned and no longer singing.

Chloe bucked him off and scrambled away. But he recovered quickly, lunging for the fallen knife as the humming returned.

"No!" Kaelyn screamed, diving for the weapon.

Her fingers closed around the handle as the boy reached for it. They grappled for control, the sharp blade dancing dangerously between them.

Searing pain exploded in Kaelyn's side. She gasped, feeling warm blood soak through her shirt. But she didn't let go.

Chloe appeared behind him and wrapped her arms around his neck in a chokehold. His grip on the knife loosened, and Kaelyn wrenched it away.

He thrashed wildly, his humming turning to wordless screams. Kaelyn backed away, clutching the knife with shaking hands. Chloe held on, her face pale from the strain.

"Hold on, girls!" Ruth's voice rang out. The older woman sprinted toward them, her face set with determination. She reached the struggling group and, without hesitation, grabbed the boy's flailing arms, pinning them to his sides. "I've got him! Don't let go, Chloe!"

Long seconds ticked by as his struggles weakened. Finally, he went limp in their arms. Ruth nodded to Chloe. "We can let go now," she said, her voice steady despite the exertion. They carefully lowered him to the ground.

"Is he . . ." Kaelyn couldn't finish the question.

Ruth pressed her fingers to the boy's neck, then shook her head. "He's gone," she said, her voice gruff but tinged with sadness. She looked at Kaelyn and Chloe. Her usual stern expression eased. "You girls okay?"

"He's dead? But why?" The adrenaline drained from Kaelyn's body, leaving her trembling and light-headed. She sank to her knees, the bloody knife falling from her grasp. "Why did he die?"

"Kaelyn!" Chloe rushed to her side. "You're hurt!"

Ruth was already kneeling beside them. "Let me see," she commanded, gently moving Chloe's hands aside.

Kaelyn looked down, surprised to see the growing bloodstain on her shirt. "Oh," she said faintly. "I guess I am."

Ruth pressed her hand against the wound, making Kaelyn wince. "It's not too deep, but we need to get it cleaned and bandaged. Can you stand, girl?"

Kaelyn nodded, trying to focus through the pain and shock. "I think so." She glanced at the boy. "I don't understand. Did I cut him?"

"No time to check right now," Ruth replied. "Chloe, help me get her up. I don't think the cut's too deep, but I want Daisy to check it."

With Ruth on one side and Chloe on the other, Kaelyn struggled to her feet. They made their way toward the main lodge, Kaelyn leaning heavily on her supporters.

"We should have had Daisy come to her," Chloe said. "Get a stretcher or something so she didn't have to walk."

"Probably right, but it's safer inside the cabin." Ruth's eyes darted around constantly, alert for any new threats. "Dick better have our place secured," she muttered. Ruth adjusted her grip on Kaelyn, urging her to keep moving.

The cabin appeared impossibly distant, each step heavy with the realization the safety they had once believed in was slipping away.

Chapter 17

As they reached the porch, the door burst open. Dick stood there, a rifle in his hands and a wild look in his eyes.

"Thank God," he breathed, lowering the weapon. "I was about to come looking for you." He stopped as he took in their disheveled appearance. "Are you guys all right?"

Ruth shook her head. "Kaelyn's hurt. The boy was a Star Bright. We had to . . . take care of it."

Dick's face hardened. "I was afraid of that. His whole family . . ." He trailed off, glancing over their heads toward the cabins. "Let's get you inside."

"You heard the man," Ruth said, urging them forward. "Inside, now. Daisy will tend to your wound properly once we're safe."

As Dick ushered them into the lodge, Kaelyn's mind reeled. In the span of a week, she'd lost her grandparents, her home, and any sense of safety she'd managed to hold on to. And now, even this refuge had been shattered.

She thought of her parents, still unreachable in Africa. Of her friends back in Cody, their fates unknown. Of the future that now seemed more uncertain than ever.

But as Chloe helped her to a chair and Ruth called for Daisy, Kaelyn set her jaw. She'd survived. She'd fought. And she would keep fighting, no matter what came next.

The world had changed, but Kaelyn was changing too. She had to if she wanted to live through this nightmare. Kaelyn made a silent vow. She would be strong. She would survive. And somehow, someway, she would find a way to make it through this disaster.

She had to. There was no other choice.

Inside the lodge, confusion reigned. People rushed back and forth, some carrying weapons, others helping the wounded. Kaelyn caught glimpses of familiar faces twisted with fear and confusion.

"What happened out there?" Dick asked, pistol in hand.

Chloe, her hands still pressed against Kaelyn's wound, gave a quick rundown of the attack.

Dick's face grew grimmer with each word.

Daisy appeared, first aid supplies in hand, wearing a face mask and heavy gloves, the kind used for washing dishes. "How bad is it?"

"Don't know," Ruth answered. "Didn't take time to check it out. We applied pressure as best we could and got to the cabin. We weren't sure if it was safe out there." She looked toward her husband. "Is it safe?"

Dick lifted his shoulders in response. "Maybe? Near as we can tell, the parents and teen boy turned," he said, shaking his head. "The mom was in their cabin, holding the younger girls. Covered in blood, the lot of them. She was singing and smiling." He swallowed hard. "The girls were dead. When we approached the mom, she took the knife to herself."

Chloe and Kaelyn gasped.

Dick gave a single nod and continued the awful story. "The dad was at the horses, humming away as he fired his gun, but the boy slipped out. I should have realized . . ."

"It's not your fault," Kaelyn said, wincing as Daisy lifted her shirt to examine the cut. "No one could have known."

Dick nodded, but the guilt in his eyes remained. "We need to do a full sweep of the property, make sure there aren't any more threats."

"We've lost people," Daisy said, gently cleaning Kaelyn's wound.

"The boy's dead too," Ruth added.

Pulling his lips tight, Dick shook his head. "I'm sorry you had to do that."

"I don't know what happened," Ruth replied. "I'm not exactly sure how or why he died. He wasn't breathing and had no pulse. Someone will need to check him."

"I'll send a team," Dick said. "What about the injured?"

Daisy shook her head. "The man got off several shots before he was stopped. Two were hit." Daisy looked at Ruth before shifting her gaze to Chloe. "You're all three covered in blood. Is it Kaelyn's, or is it . . . is it from the Star Bright?"

Kaelyn looked at Chloe, who was staring at her hands. Shaking her head, she said, "Probably from Kaelyn and the boy."

"Me too," Kaelyn muttered.

"Ruth?" Daisy asked.

"What?" Ruth said gruffly. "We did what we had to do. You're a retired nurse, right? You've seen these kinds of things before."

Daisy was shaking her head. "School nurse. I mean, I'm an RN, but I worked the last twenty years in schools."

Dick stepped toward his wife and reached out his hand.

"Don't touch her!" Daisy yelled. "She could be contaminated."

Dick jumped back. "Sorry. I forgot what you told us."

"What did she tell you?" Chloe asked, glancing between Daisy and Dick.

"We don't know how it spreads," Daisy said. "The sickness. It could be airborne, or it could be passed through blood."

"Pshaw." Ruth shook her head. "I'm sure these girls are fine."

"Well, I'm not. I'm not sure any of you are fine."

"What about the others?" Kaelyn asked, her voice small and timid. "Did they have blood on them?"

"The mother and her girls, yes," Dick said. "Daisy told us not to touch them."

"Not without wearing gloves and taking precautions. Same with the husband. And the boy, where is he?"

Ruth described where they left him. Dick said they'd move the family together. "I'll get someone on that."

"No, Dick," Daisy said. "You'll stay right here. If Kaelyn, Chloe, or Ruth start humming . . ." Her voice faded away.

Kaelyn's heart rate sped up. "What do you mean if we start humming? I'm not a Star Bright. I'm not."

"Hold still," Daisy ordered.

"Why are you treating us like this?" Chloe's voice was higher pitched than usual. "We're the victims here. He attacked us."

"I understand," Daisy said, her voice calm and soothing. "You need to remain calm. You're probably right, and it's nothing, but I'm sure you understand we can't risk it. We've already lost another man and have two people injured. We can't risk— "

"I'm not a Star Bright." Chloe's voice was fierce, her eyes flashing.

Daisy turned to Dick. "I think we need to put some protocols into place. Safety protocols. New people need to be put in quarantine. Maybe . . . maybe those cabins you have? The ones that are walk-in only."

Dick nodded. "The two off-grid cabins? It's a good idea. How long?"

Shaking her head and shrugging at the same time, Daisy sighed. "Two weeks? I don't know. I'm only guessing based on standard incubations." She dropped her shoulders. "Kaelyn, Chloe, and Ruth need to go into quarantine too."

Ruth leveled a hard stare at Daisy. "You can't be serious."

"I am serious. Until we know how it spreads, we need to take all the precautions."

"Who'll handle the kitchen? The . . . the . . . everything?"

"We'll figure it out. And your clothes need to be disposed of. Burned."

Dick took a step toward his wife, but Daisy shook her head. "Wait until she gets cleaned up. You'll be able to chastely say goodbye. No kissing."

Ruth shook her head. "Seems a little ridiculous, but I guess you are the nurse here. The *school* nurse."

"I want to keep everyone safe, exactly as you do," Daisy said, then turned to Kaelyn. "This isn't too bad. It isn't deep. It's long, though. I'm going to use the butterfly bandages to close it."

"You don't even know what causes the . . . the sickness," Chloe said. "How can you say we need to be locked up when you don't know?"

"Probably another plandemic," Dick muttered, earning him a dirty look from Chloe and a hard stare from his wife.

"You're right," Daisy agreed. "We don't know. But we must do what we can to keep everyone safe. It's only for two weeks."

Chloe murmured words that made Kaelyn blush.

After the bandaging was complete, which was awkward with Daisy's extra thick gloves on, she said, "Let's get you all settled. I'll have someone grab your clothes and bring them to you. Kaelyn, are you well enough to walk?"

Chloe began to argue that she wanted to pack her own things after she cleaned up, but Daisy said, "We're going to do this my way. As Ruth said, I'm the retired RN. It's my job to keep everyone medically safe. Dick? I want you to find my husband and choose another man. Not your son, someone else. Someone who doesn't know them well."

"I'm sure we don't need help."

Daisy leveled her gaze at him as she moved her hand to the pistol on her hip. "I'm sure you're right, but we'll do it my way."

A few minutes later, with tears streaming down her face from both the pain of her injury and the frustration of the situation, Kaelyn leaned heavily on Chloe as they made their way to the isolated cabin. Could she have been contaminated? Would she, Chloe, and Ruth all start humming and become Star Brights?

Chapter 18

Kaelyn stood in the doorway of the off-grid cabin, her side throbbing. The small, rustic structure loomed before her like a prison cell. No electricity. No running water. Just four walls and a roof to keep them isolated from the rest of the lodge.

"Well, don't stand there gawking," Ruth grumbled, pushing past her. "Let's see what our jailers have done with the place. Probably added chains and bars."

Chloe placed a gentle hand on Kaelyn's shoulder. "You okay?"

Kaelyn nodded, not trusting her voice. They stepped inside, the floorboards creaking under their feet.

The cabin wasn't anything like she'd expected. When they'd said it was an off-grid cabin, she thought it would be sparse. While it wasn't overly decorated, she was surprised to see how comfortable it looked. The kitchen and living room were one big open space. A small table with four chairs sat in the center, and a woodstove squatted in the corner. There were two doors at the back and a ladder-style staircase going up to a loft space.

Outside, Daisy's voice carried through the open door. "Remember, stay inside or use the private courtyard or upstairs balcony only. We'll bring drinking water and food."

"We're not prisoners!" Chloe called back, anger coloring her words.

"No, you're not," Daisy replied, her tone maddeningly calm. "But until we know how this thing spreads, we can't take any chances. Ruth, will you be sure to show them how the water and bathroom work? The lighting?"

"Of course I will."

"I want you to take off your clothes," Daisy instructed. "Put them over the fence in the back, and we'll take care of them."

"Burn them, you mean?" Chloe clarified, a snap still in her tone.

"Yes. That's exactly what I mean," Daisy replied. "Try not to get blood on anything."

Kaelyn turned to look at Daisy. "How long do we have to stay here?"

"Two weeks, give or take. We'll be setting up a guard schedule— "

"That won't be necessary," Ruth interrupted. "We're not going anywhere."

"It's not only to keep you in," Daisy explained. "It's to keep others out. And . . . to watch for any changes in your condition."

The implication hung heavy in the air. They were being quarantined, yes, but they were also being observed. Like lab rats. Or ticking time bombs.

"We need to let the other lodges know about the new procedures," Dick's voice joined the conversation. "All new arrivals will need to be quarantined."

"Where?" Ruth asked. "We only have two of these cabins."

"We can set up some canvas outfitter tents," Dick replied. "We'll put them where we planned to build the three additional off-grid cabins. The areas are already cleared. We can put the tents there for now."

"And when winter comes?" Ruth challenged.

There was a pause before Dick answered. "Let's hope we're not dealing with this by then."

Hope. Kaelyn almost laughed. Hope seemed in short supply these days.

"All right," Daisy said. "Your clothes are on the way. Clean up as best you can with the rain barrel water. I'll have someone bring food and drinking water soon."

Dick paused at the threshold of the door, his eyes locking onto his wife of who knew how many years. Kaelyn guessed, based on the age of their son, that they'd been married about as long as her grandparents had. Fresh tears rose to the surface at the thought.

"I love you, you know," Dick said, his voice husky.

"Right back at you, old man," Ruth replied, a small smile playing on her lips. "Will you have Brian stop by? I'd like to talk to him."

After glancing behind him to see Daisy's response, Dick turned back. "I'll have him help bring the things you'll need."

Footsteps retreated, leaving the three women alone in their new prison.

Ruth immediately began moving about the cabin, muttering under her breath. "Don't touch anything," she cautioned. "Don't want Nurse Ratched getting all bent out of shape."

Chloe and Kaelyn shared a look and a shrug.

Kaelyn's eyes stung with unshed tears. Her grandfather was barely in the ground, and here she was, locked away like a criminal. Or worse, like a disease.

"Hey," Chloe said softly. "we'll get through this. It's a precaution."

"But what if— " Kaelyn's voice cracked. "What if we *are* infected? What if we turn into . . . into them?"

"We won't," Chloe said firmly, but Kaelyn could hear the doubt beneath her words.

"All right, listen up," Ruth's sharp voice cut through their moment. "I know this situation is less than ideal, but we're not going to spend the next two weeks wallowing in self-pity. We need to make the best of it."

"How?" Kaelyn asked, hating how small her voice sounded.

"First, we clean ourselves up. There's an outdoor shower, fed by a rain barrel. There're robes in the closet. We'll use those until our clothes arrive. I'll also show you how to use the bathroom. It's a compost toilet, so you'll need to follow the instructions."

"Eww." Chloe made a face.

"What's a compost toilet?" Kaelyn asked.

"Waterless toilet," Ruth said simply. "When we built these cabins, we wanted to do something different, offer people a peek at a unique way of life. That and they were too far from our main lodge to put in the amenities needed, like electricity and water. Plus, we didn't want to dig another sewer. The compost toilet uses wood shavings. Come on. I'll show you."

Ruth led them to the bathroom. At first glance, it seemed like a regular, compact bathroom. But closer inspection allowed Kaelyn to see the differences between this bathroom and the one she used in the lodge.

The faucet sink was small, and Ruth pointed out the foot pedal. "There's a container under the sink. Use the pedal to bring up the water." She demonstrated the process. "There's no hot and cold. You get what you get. The kitchen sink is set up exactly the same. If you want hot water, you need to warm it."

The small shower was also without regular plumbing—just a bag hanging above it. The toilet was odd shaped, more of a box with a toilet lid on it. And there was no handle to flush.

"We call it a compost toilet, though that's not entirely accurate." Ruth lifted the lid. "Composting doesn't actually take place in the toilet. This is simply a collection device. The toilet material is taken outside to a compost bin . . ." She crinkled her brow. "I suppose that's something we'll need to mention. Someone else will need to dump our bucket."

Chloe was again making a face and shaking her head. "So gross."

Ruth shrugged. "If we do it right, by following the rules written here— " she pointed to a paper on the wall " — there will be no odor. Excrement can be recycled by composting. Composting itself won't happen here, but we'll start the process by using a cover material."

She gestured toward a short metal bucket with a lid. "That's sawdust. After you do your business, you'll sprinkle sawdust over it, making sure it's covered. Doing this will make it odor free. This is simply a bucket. When it's full, we'll add a lid to carry it to the compost bin. Well, someone else will."

Chloe was still shaking her head. "I can't even . . ."

"Well, you will. We'll keep the jug under the sink full so we can wash up in the sink. The indoor shower uses a camp shower bag. We'll fill it with water and set it out in the sun to warm. We'll need to heat the water today, since we should shower now instead of waiting for the sun to warm it."

Kaelyn had used a camping shower before when she and her folks had gone on a weeklong camping trip in the national forest. It was fine, as long as you were quick and didn't try to wash your hair.

"Now let's go look at the outdoor shower," Ruth said.

Kaelyn and Chloe dutifully followed behind, Chloe still shaking her head while carrying the shower bag.

The outdoor shower was set up in a private courtyard off the bedroom. There was a bench outside the enclosed shower and a second bench inside. "This is hooked directly to one of the rain barrels." She showed them how it worked by twisting a knob.

"The kitchen sink is connected to a second barrel, giving us wash water inside. We could drink the water, too, but we'd want to filter it first. Usually, we bring drinking water from the main lodge to people staying here. Why don't you two take turns at this shower. I'll use the camp shower inside. Kaelyn, you need to be extra careful not to get your wound wet. Maybe do some sort of sponge bath." Her face crinkled, showing the deep lines of experience and a lifetime of hard work. "I can help you if you need it."

Kaelyn shook her head, her cheeks warming at the thought of needing help to shower. "No. No, that's fine. I can do it. Do you have a plastic bag I can put over my cast?"

"I'm sure I can find you something to use. Let's get on with it. There are towels and washcloths in the closet by the door. That's where the robes are too. There's another linen closet by the bathroom. I'll gather my things there after I get the water warmed. We've got a propane stove, so it'll work quickly. Any questions?"

After a moment of silence, they shook their heads, and Ruth disappeared into the house.

"Can you believe that toilet?" Chloe shuddered. "So disgusting."

"It's not too bad," Kaelyn responded, thinking of times she'd gone in the woods after digging what was commonly referred to as a "cat hole" and leaning against a tree.

The look on Chloe's face was pure disbelief. "Let me wash my hands, and you can shower first. You've got more blood on you than I do. I'll go see if Ruth found a bag for your arm. Remember what she said about your knife wound."

Ruth appeared with a plastic grocery bag. Chloe volunteered to get the towels, washcloths, and bathrobes. "Why don't you get started? Throw your clothes over the fence like Daisy said and get in the shower. Once you're in, I'll hang what you need on the hooks right here." She motioned to the hooks by the door. "And I'll hand in a washcloth for you."

While the shower wasn't exactly warm, it wasn't cold either. Keeping the injury dry was awkward, especially with the bag over her arm and the cast making her extra clumsy, but Kaelyn found the water sufficient to not only get clean but to also hide her tears. Tears for the absence of her parents, the death of her grandparents, and the incident this morning.

The boy, who she'd never even met after his family arrived, wasn't any older than she was. How did he and his parents all turn into Star Brights? Were the younger children also afflicted? She hated to even think about what happened in the cabin of horrors.

And why did he die? He sliced her with the knife, but as far as she knew, she hadn't cut him. Ruth and Chloe had held him but not in such a way as to cut off his air supply or anything like that. With the concerns over the spread of the illness, she couldn't imagine Daisy or anyone else would want to give him much of an examination. Would they ever know how he died?

Clean and wrapped in a robe, Kaelyn went into the main room of the cabin while Chloe showered. She felt marginally better, but the gnawing fear in her gut remained.

Ruth was already finished and in clean clothes instead of a robe. "They stopped by with our things." She pointed to Kaelyn's backpack. "Not everything, but enough to get us by for a few days. Brian said he'd bring more as we need it. They brought us sandwiches too. Did you get your bandage wet?"

"I don't think so. I was careful."

"Better let me look at it anyway. Daisy sent over a well-stocked first aid kit. Plenty of bandages for you." She scrunched her lips. "Brian collected all the knives when he was here. I told him if one of us happened to be a Star Bright, we'd most certainly figure out how to get the job done, knives or no knives."

"I'm not a Star Bright." Kaelyn shook her head.

"Tell them, not me."

After checking the bandage and declaring it satisfactory, Ruth said, "I wonder what's keeping Chloe?" The words were barely out of her mouth when they heard the door to the courtyard open.

Rubbing her hair with a towel, Chloe entered the room. "The water pressure leaves a bit to be desired."

"At least you're clean," Ruth said. "Let's eat."

They ate in silence, as the gravity of their situation settled over them. Kaelyn nibbled at her food, her appetite gone.

"Eat," Ruth commanded. "You need to keep up your strength."

"Why?" Kaelyn muttered. "So I can be strong when I turn into a monster?"

Ruth's hand slammed down on the table, making Kaelyn and Chloe jump. "Enough of that kind of talk. We are not going to sit here and feel sorry for ourselves. We are not going to give up before anything's even happened. Do you understand me?"

Kaelyn nodded, tears pricking at her eyes.

"Good. Now, here's how this is going to work. We're going to treat these two weeks like a job. We'll set up a schedule. Cleaning, organizing . . . we'll do calisthenics if we have to. Anything to keep our minds and bodies occupied."

"And if we start changing?" Chloe asked hesitantly.

Ruth's face hardened. "We'll deal with that if it happens. Until it does, we act as if we're walking out of here in two weeks, right as rain. Got it?"

Both Kaelyn and Chloe nodded.

"All right," Ruth said, her tone softening slightly. "Finish your lunch. Then we'll figure out sleeping arrangements."

As they ate, Kaelyn's mind wandered to her parents again. Were they safe? Did they get her emails? She wished she could email them, if nothing else, so she could get her feelings out. Maybe she'd write things down. She noticed a small notepad on the desk in the corner, or her notebook might be in her backpack. If not, she'd ask them to bring it next time.

She thought about her grandparents. What would they think of all this? Grandma Joyce would probably say it was all part of God's plan, even if they couldn't understand it.

Grandpa Terry would tell her to keep her chin up and her eyes open.

After lunch, Ruth made room assignments. She claimed the room with the courtyard while Kaelyn and Chloe would sleep upstairs. "There're twin beds. Plus, you have the small balcony."

They took their bags upstairs, each choosing a bed. Chloe walked to the French door, opening it to the outside. The balcony wasn't much. Just enough to step out. It was so narrow it wouldn't even hold a chair. "Seems kind of useless," Chloe muttered.

"The creek sounds nice," Kaelyn added.

"I guess." Chloe shrugged, her hand going to her stomach. "Ugh. That lunch isn't sitting well."

"Are you sick to your stomach?"

"A little. It's just . . . it's the baby."

"Morning sickness? It's afternoon."

"Doesn't matter. I'm going to change into some clothes and lie down. You might want to do the same. You heard Ruth, she's going to find things to keep us busy. Take advantage of today while she's still thinking of what we can do while we're serving our sentence. Oh, and by the way, don't go turning into one of those Star Brights. I won't hesitate to fight for my life and the life of my baby."

Chapter 19

The balcony door was fully open, letting in the crisp mountain air and the soothing sounds of the nearby creek. Kaelyn sat in the chair she'd pulled nearby, her journal open on her lap. Tomorrow marked the end of their two-week quarantine, and she was reflecting on the experience.

Despite the initial shock and fear, the past days hadn't been as terrible as she'd first imagined. Kaelyn thought back to their first night in the cabin, how overwhelming it had felt to be locked away from the world. She remembered the panic that had gripped her, the fear they might be forgotten or abandoned. But as the days passed, they had found a rhythm, a way to cope with their new reality.

The biggest challenge had been the isolation while she was grieving. Cut off from the rest of the community, with only Ruth and Chloe for company, Kaelyn had struggled with feelings of loneliness and disconnection. She had overcome this by creating routines, by finding ways to stay busy and engaged. Ruth's insistence on keeping them active had been a lifesaver, giving structure to their days and purpose to their actions.

Another hurdle had been adapting to the off-grid lifestyle. Used to the conveniences of modern life, Kaelyn had initially found it frustrating to manage without electricity or proper running water. But as they learned to work with what they had, she discovered a newfound appreciation for the simple things.

She'd been concerned they might run out of water, but there'd been several gentle rains and one gully washer, as Ruth called it, while they were in quarantine. She particularly enjoyed the peacefulness of evenings lit by lantern light. They'd play a game or take turns reading aloud. But they never stayed up terribly late. Ruth made a point of saying it was important for them to allow their bodies to adjust to working with the sun and sleeping with the dark.

Each morning at breakfast, Ruth read a Bible verse. At first, Chloe seemed almost angry about it, but in recent days, Kaelyn noticed a shift. The young widow had started asking questions about the meaning of certain passages and how they might relate to their situation.

One morning, she wondered if Ruth had chosen a verse on perseverance for a reason, musing aloud about its lesson for their small group. Another time, Chloe asked about the historical context of a parable, curious how it applied to their lives now.

Kaelyn even shared how her grandparents had told the story of Jacob before leaving Cody, which led to a reading from Genesis and reinforced Ruth's earlier discussion on perseverance. Chloe's growing interest in the readings deepened their conversations, drawing everyone into discussions that stretched well past breakfast.

Around midmorning, Brian, Dick, or Daisy brought them food and supplies, leaving them on the front porch. They'd stay to visit, never coming inside but talking through screened windows, staying several feet away. They'd tried to keep the quarantine group informed about the goings-on in the community.

During these visits, Kaelyn learned about the efforts to fortify the lodge and surrounding areas. Dick had shared details about new security measures being implemented, including regular patrols and an early warning system for approaching vehicles or large groups. Brian had talked about plans to expand their food production, with new gardens being planted and discussions about acquiring additional livestock. They were even planning to live-capture wild rabbits and turkeys to try and domesticate them.

Daisy, ever the medical professional, kept them updated on health-related matters. She spoke of ongoing efforts to understand the Star Bright phenomenon. While information was becoming spotty, they could still get on the internet most days. Daisy was particularly concerned about the lack of information being shared by the CDC. There'd been no recent updates or announcements about the vaccine being formulated.

According to Daisy, it was almost like the CDC and others had given up. Even the information being shared by regular people had decreased. Sometimes she'd find an article and it would change while she was reading it. The screen would blip and that was it. Same with videos. "If I didn't know better," Daisy had said, "I'd think we were in the book *1984.*"

Daisy's observation about the similarities between the current world and George Orwell's historical novel prompted Ruth to add it to their reading list. A copy rested in the lodge's small library, and Dick brought it the next time he visited. Kaelyn had never read it before, but as Ruth read aloud, the parallels Daisy had pointed out became clear to her.

Kaelyn knew a mother and her daughter occupied the cabin next door, and a third group was staying in one of the canvas tents that had been set up. She'd even managed to have a few conversations with the pair in the neighboring cabin from her balcony perch.

These conversations had become a bright spot in Kaelyn's days. They had been on a camping trip when everything fell apart. They shared stories of their journey to the lodge and explained their request to stay until things improved, as their home was in Ohio.

Ruth had been consulted about her thoughts on the mother and daughter remaining, even though they didn't have a connection to the lodge. Her vote had been yes, especially when she found out the woman had lost her husband to cancer the summer before. "Look after orphans and widows in their distress," she'd said.

Kaelyn experienced a pang in her chest at Ruth's words. She wasn't an orphan, but the sting of loss lingered, making her feel like one. The idea of caring for others who had lost so much resonated with her. She understood how tough it could be to lose someone you loved, and like Ruth, she wanted to help those who were hurting.

That morning, Dick was the one to bring things. He asked to speak privately with Ruth. They went to the bedroom window.

Kaelyn busied herself dusting the main living space, inching closer to the bedroom. Chloe, meanwhile, decided to reorganize their shelf of games and books, located near the bedroom door. Both of them hoped to overhear part of the hushed discussion. Kaelyn's stomach knotted with anxiety, while Chloe nervously rubbed her growing belly.

As they heard Ruth's footsteps approaching the door, Kaelyn quickly moved to the couch, pretending to fluff the pillows. Chloe swiftly returned to the kitchen area, opening a cupboard as if searching for something. Both tried to appear nonchalant, though their hearts raced with anticipation.

When Ruth emerged from the bedroom with a strained expression, Kaelyn asked, "What's wrong? Did something happen at the lodge?"

"Is everyone okay?" Chloe added, her voice filled with concern.

"Brian's gone."

"Gone! Did he— "

"No! I mean gone to Casper. He went after his family. Things are even worse down there than here. While we still have electricity at the lodge and cabins, thanks mainly to the solar system and backup generator, commercial power is failing. Everything is deteriorating. He should have gone weeks ago."

Kaelyn nodded in relief. Everyone knew he was worried about his kids. With communication becoming so difficult, he'd become even more frantic. Kaelyn's thoughts drifted to her parents. She'd asked Brian to use her laptop to email them, hoping somehow the message would get through. He'd checked a few times, but there had been no reply. Logically, Kaelyn knew sending an email or text herself wouldn't make any difference, but the burning need to reach out persisted.

She glanced at her phone, plugged into a portable charger. The others had been helping Kaelyn and Chloe keep their phones charged, as they used them for timekeeping. This far from the lodge there was no service of any kind, but it was comforting to have the devices working, if only for offline things. Ruth, on the other hand, had requested a windup alarm clock, claiming she didn't miss her flip phone at all. Ruth didn't have regular cell service, she just bought time with a card at the local superstore.

A smile tugged at Kaelyn's lips as she remembered Ruth's response when Chloe had commented how only serial killers used throwaway phones like hers. The older woman had simply raised an eyebrow and said, "And? Your point?" It was the first glimpse of humor Kaelyn had seen from Ruth.

During their time in quarantine, Kaelyn had come to appreciate Ruth's no-nonsense approach to their situation. The woman was far from the warm, loving presence Grandma Joyce had been, but there was an undeniable kindness beneath her gruff exterior. Ruth had insisted on keeping them busy, even arranging for mending and sewing projects to be brought in.

Kaelyn's pen moved across the page of her journal as she recalled their progression from simple tasks, like sewing on buttons and adding patches, to more complex projects. Daisy had initially hesitated to provide scissors, worried they may become a weapon should one of the women turn into a Star Bright, but eventually, she relented and gave them a round-tipped pair.

They started working on repurposing clothing gathered from all three lodges, items brought by community members or left behind by guests. Anything beyond repair was being cut into smaller pieces for quilts or other projects.

Her writing paused as she thought about Chloe. The pregnant woman's morning sickness had improved over the past week, and she was starting to show a little. Kaelyn had noticed the gentle swell of Chloe's belly and the way her hands often rested protectively over it when she thought no one was looking.

Chloe's pregnancy had become a source of both joy and sorrow in their little group. There was excitement about new life, a symbol of hope in their uncertain world. But it was also a constant reminder of what Chloe had lost. Kaelyn had overheard her crying softly at night, whispering to her unborn child about the father they would never know.

The grief was intense, a heavy presence that sometimes threatened to overwhelm their small living space. But Chloe was strong. Kaelyn had watched her push through the pain, focusing on preparing for her baby's arrival. She'd even started crocheting a small blanket, her fingers working the hook with determination as she spoke of her plans and hopes for the future.

Kaelyn set her pen down and took a deep breath. She thought about how much she had changed over the past two weeks. At the beginning of their quarantine, she had felt completely lost, like everything was too much to handle.

But slowly, she had started to find her groove. She set to organizing their limited supplies and even came up with an inventory system Ruth actually liked. There was also the day she figured out how to fix the foot pump for their kitchen water when it stopped working.

There were emotional changes too. Kaelyn noticed she was speaking up more, sharing her thoughts and ideas instead of fading into the background. She had even become a kind of peacemaker between Ruth and Chloe, stepping in to help when things got tense in their cramped space. They might seem like small things, but they were a sign of growth, and Kaelyn felt proud.

She'd promised herself she would be strong, the kind of person her grandma would have wanted her to be. It wasn't always easy, but she was trying. Each day, she found herself a little more confident, a little more capable of facing their new reality.

A sound from outside caught Kaelyn's attention. She stepped out onto the tiny balcony and leaned against the railing. But as her toe caught on the slight change in the flooring, she stumbled, her heart leaping into her throat. She lurched forward, her hand shooting out to grab the railing just in time. The edge of the balcony seemed too close, and for a moment, the ground below felt impossibly far.

"Good job, Kaelyn," she muttered. "Sailing over the edge wouldn't have ended well."

Shaking off the feeling, she steadied herself and refocused on the forest across the creek. Was that movement she saw? She strained her eyes, trying to make out shapes in the dense summer foliage.

The forest was a tapestry of greens, from the deep, almost black shadows beneath the pines to the bright, sunlit leaves of the aspens. The afternoon light filtered through the canopy, creating a dappled pattern on the forest floor. Kaelyn scanned the underbrush, her eyes catching on every shifting shadow and swaying branch.

Yesterday, when their food was delivered, they'd been told someone had spotted a cow and calf moose in the area. Could it be them? Or maybe a deer or elk? Kaelyn focused intently on the spot where she thought she'd seen movement. Bison was also a possibility. They were known to frequent the area. Could it be a bear? Either grizzly or black bears were possible in the area, a thought that sent a small shiver of excitement and fear down her spine.

The creek burbled, its constant flow a soothing backdrop to the rustling leaves and occasional birdsong. Kaelyn breathed deeply, savoring the scent of pine and clean mountain air. For a moment, she could almost forget the troubles of the world and lose herself in the timeless beauty of the wilderness.

For several minutes, she stood perfectly still, watching and waiting. She thought she caught another flicker of motion, but it was gone as quickly as it appeared. Eventually, with a mixture of disappointment and lingering curiosity, Kaelyn returned to her chair. She picked up her journal again, ready to continue documenting her thoughts and experiences.

As she settled back into writing, a sense of anticipation began to build. Tomorrow, their quarantine would end. Whatever came next, she was determined to face it with the strength and resilience that would make her grandparents proud. The world outside might still be uncertain and dangerous, but Kaelyn Fisher was ready to meet it head-on.

Yet, as much as she longed for freedom, she couldn't help but feel a twinge of anxiety. What would life be like back at the lodge? How much had changed in their absence? She worried about integrating back into the larger group, about the potential dangers lurking beyond their safe little bubble.

There were practical concerns too. Would they have to take on more responsibilities? Kaelyn thought about the patrols Dick had talked about and the ongoing work to keep their community safe. She had previously been excused from shifts at the roadblock because of the cast on her arm, but once it was removed, she'd be part of the security team.

Daisy mentioned they might have to take the cast off themselves, but she didn't think it was time yet. Ideally, she would have x-rays to see how her arm was healing, but that wasn't going to happen.

The idea of removing the cast was both exciting and scary. Without it, she could do a lot more, and part of her was eager to help out and show she was useful. But another part of her was terrified of facing the tough realities of their new world. The cast had been a convenient excuse to avoid the hard stuff, and she wasn't sure she was ready to give that up.

And what about the future beyond tomorrow? Kaelyn's mind wandered to the bigger questions looming on the horizon. Would they stay at the lodge indefinitely? Was there a chance of rebuilding some semblance of a normal life? And always, always, the thought of her parents lingered. Were they safe? Would she ever see them again?

Despite the uncertainties, she felt a flicker of hope. They had survived this far. They had adapted and grown stronger. And maybe they could build something good out of the ruins of the old world.

With renewed determination, Kaelyn bent over her journal once more. Tomorrow would come, with all its unknowns. But for now, she had her thoughts to order, her experiences to record. In the simple act of writing, she found purpose and calm. It was a small thing, perhaps, but it was hers. And in a world where so much had been taken away, that meant everything.

Chapter 20

Kaelyn descended the ladder-like stairs from the loft, her mind again on the movement she thought she'd seen across the creek. She would've loved to have seen a pair of moose. Even bighorn sheep would've been a welcome sight. She'd make a point of looking for them later.

The cabin's main room was filled with the aroma of Ruth's cooking.

"Perfect timing," Ruth said, not looking up from the stove. "Lunch is almost ready."

Kaelyn inhaled deeply, savoring the comforting smell of home-cooked food. After two weeks of simple meals and limited ingredients, even the most basic dishes seemed like a feast.

Chloe sat at the table, absently rubbing her belly. "Did you see anything interesting up there?" she asked.

Kaelyn hesitated, considering how to describe what she'd seen or thought she'd seen. The memory already felt hazy, like a half-remembered dream. "I thought I saw something move across the creek, but I couldn't be sure. Maybe it was the moose pair they told us about yesterday."

Chloe's eyes lit up with interest. "Moose? That would be something to see. I've never seen one in the wild before."

As they settled in for lunch, a comfortable silence fell over the cabin. Kaelyn found herself hyper-aware of every sound. The clink of utensils against plates, Chloe's soft chewing, the distant rush of the creek outside. It was their last full day of quarantine, and she felt a mixture of anticipation and anxiety buzzing just beneath her skin.

"So," Chloe said, breaking the quiet, "what do you think you'll do first when we're out of here?"

Kaelyn paused, her fork halfway to her mouth. She'd been avoiding thinking too much about life after quarantine, but now the question loomed large. She shook her head, considering. "I don't know. Maybe try to contact my parents again? I know Brian was checking my email, but . . ."

"But it's not the same as doing it yourself," Chloe finished, nodding in understanding.

A lump formed in Kaelyn's throat. "Yeah. I need to know if they're okay, you know? Even if I can't reach them, at least I'll feel like I'm doing something."

Chloe reached across the table and squeezed her hand. "I get it. It's hard not knowing."

"What about you?" Kaelyn asked.

Chloe hesitated, clearing her throat. Her eyes flicked to Ruth before returning to Kaelyn. When she spoke, her voice was low, as if she was afraid of her own words. "I've been thinking maybe I should try to get to Colorado. See about getting fuel and heading out. Go to my family."

Kaelyn's stomach dropped as though the floor had suddenly given way. "What? No. It's not safe out there. And what about the baby?"

"I know it's risky," Chloe admitted. She took her hand away from Kaelyn's and moved it protectively over her belly. "But I can't shake the feeling I should be with my family. They must be worried sick about me."

Panic rose in Kaelyn's chest. She couldn't imagine facing this new world without Chloe by her side. "But we don't even know how things are . . . if where your parents live is still . . ." She couldn't bring herself to finish the thought.

Chloe's eyes flashed. "If it's still what? Still standing? Still full of normal people? You think because we had a few incidents, the whole country has gone to ruin? I'm sure there are places like here, where they've joined together for safety."

Kaelyn flinched at Chloe's tone, hurt and anger bubbling up inside her. "That's not what I meant. It could be dangerous."

"Life is dangerous now, Kaelyn," Chloe snapped. "We can't hide in cabins forever."

"I'm not hiding," Kaelyn protested, her voice rising slightly. "I'm trying to be smart. To survive."

"And I'm trying to take care of myself. Of my unborn child," Chloe shot back. "You of all people should understand."

The words hit Kaelyn like a slap. "What's that supposed to mean?"

"It means you're not the only one who's lost people," Chloe said, her voice thick with emotion. "At least your parents are still out there somewhere."

Kaelyn felt tears pricking at her eyes, both anger and guilt washing over her. "You don't know that. They could be . . ."

"Enough!" Ruth's sharp voice cut through their argument. "What in the world has gotten into you two?"

Before either of them could respond, there was a commotion outside. The cabin door burst open with a bang, causing all three women to jump. Two armed guards rushed in, surgical masks covering their faces, their weapons raised and ready.

"Everyone freeze!" one of them shouted. "Hands where we can see them!"

Kaelyn's heart raced as she slowly raised her hands, lunch churning in her stomach. She saw Chloe and Ruth doing the same out of the corner of her eye. The guards scanned the room.

"What's going on?" Ruth demanded, her voice steady despite the circumstances.

The second guard, a woman with short-cropped hair, spoke up. "We heard raised voices. Thought we might have a situation."

Understanding dawned on Kaelyn, horror replacing her fear. They thought one of them might have turned into a Star Bright. The reality of their situation, the constant threat they lived under, came crashing down on her with renewed force.

"It's nothing like that," Chloe said quickly. "We were having a . . . a disagreement."

The first guard, a tall man with a thick beard poking out from his mask, lowered his weapon slightly. "You're sure? No one's feeling . . . musical?"

Despite the tension of the moment, Kaelyn laughed at the absurdity of the question.

"The only thing I feel like singing is a lament for common sense," Ruth grumbled. "Now, if you don't mind, we'd appreciate it if you'd stop pointing those things at us."

The guards exchanged a look before slowly lowering their weapons. Kaelyn could see the conflict on their faces. The desire to be thorough warred with embarrassment at their overreaction.

"Sorry for the intrusion," the woman said. "We have to be cautious."

As the guards retreated, closing the door behind them, an awkward silence fell over the cabin. Kaelyn couldn't bring herself to look at Chloe, shame and embarrassment washing over her. The absurdity of their argument, amplified by the guards' dramatic entrance, seemed to press down on all of them.

Ruth cleared her throat. "Well, that was exciting. Now, what is *actually* going on?"

Kaelyn's words came out in a whisper. "I think it's too dangerous. We don't know what's out there."

"And you're right to be concerned," Ruth said. "But Chloe's also right. We can't stay hidden away forever."

"So, you think she should go?" Kaelyn asked, surprised.

Ruth shook her head. "I didn't say that. I think it's a decision that needs a lot more thought and planning. But that's not the issue here, is it?"

Kaelyn finally looked up, confused. "What do you mean?"

"I mean," Ruth said, her voice softening, "this isn't really about Chloe leaving. It's about you being afraid of losing someone else."

The words hit Kaelyn like a punch to the gut. Tears welled up in her eyes, but she blinked hard, trying to hold them back. Ruth had cut straight to the heart of her fear, laying it bare for all to see.

A gentler look settled over Chloe's face. "Oh, Kaelyn. I'm sorry. I didn't think . . ."

"No, I'm sorry," Kaelyn said, her voice barely above a whisper. "I shouldn't have reacted like that. Of course you want to be with your parents. I know I do."

Chloe reached across the table, taking Kaelyn's hand. "And I shouldn't have snapped at you about your parents. I'm sorry I was so cruel."

As they clasped hands, some of the tension left Kaelyn. When they looked at each other again, both of them had tears in their eyes.

"Look at us," Chloe said with a watery chuckle. "Getting all worked up and scaring the guards. We must look pretty silly."

Kaelyn couldn't help but laugh. "Yeah, I bet we gave them quite a fright. 'Oh no, they're arguing! Must be turning into singing psychopaths!'"

Even Ruth cracked a smile. "Well, if you two are done with the dramatics, we should probably finish our lunch. No sense in letting good food go to waste."

As they returned to their meals, Kaelyn straightened, the tension easing from her shoulders. The argument wasn't resolved, not really, but at least they had cleared the air. She knew there would be more discussions and more decisions to make, but for now, it was enough to know they cared for each other.

The rest of the afternoon passed quietly. Kaelyn found herself stealing glances at Chloe, wondering if she would actually try to leave for her parents' home. The thought of her leaving was scary, not only because she'd lose another person, as Ruth said, but because of the danger. Yet she knew she couldn't let fear control her actions or her relationships.

Before supper, Kaelyn returned to the loft, drawn once again to the small balcony. She looked out over the creek, searching for any sign of the movement she'd seen earlier. The forest was quiet, offering no answers to the questions swirling in her mind.

Tomorrow, their quarantine would end. What would await them outside? How much had changed in two weeks? And most importantly, would she have the courage to face it all without letting her fears hold her back?

With a deep breath, Kaelyn turned away from the balcony. Whatever came next, she would face it with the strength her grandparents had always believed she possessed. And this time, she wouldn't let her timidity and self-doubt get in the way.

Chapter 21

Kaelyn jolted awake, her heart pounding. The loft was shrouded in darkness; the only sound was her own rapid breathing. What had woken her? She lay still, every muscle tense, straining her ears for any unusual noise. The cabin creaked and settled around her, but nothing seemed out of the ordinary.

She glanced toward Chloe's bed, barely visible in the gloom. The other woman's steady breathing was reassuring. *Maybe it was a dream*, Kaelyn thought. *The kind that jolts you awake but fades quickly, leaving only a vague sense of unease.*

As her heartbeat steadied, she closed her eyes and tried to will herself back to sleep. How close was it to morning and the end of quarantine? She should get some rest while she still could.

They had kept themselves occupied during quarantine, but returning to the lodge meant diving into a mountain of work. Ruth was already talking about the need to start preserving food. With the garden nearly ready, their days would only get busier. Kaelyn remembered arriving at the lodge and finding Ruth already focused on preserving eggs.

Ruth explained eggs were seasonal. The chickens' production was stimulated by daylight. Hens were most productive during the spring and summer months when there was more daylight, and production slowed down in the colder months when there was less.

They had a hen who'd already hatched out babies, and two more were broody and sitting on eggs when Kaelyn went into quarantine. Had those eggs hatched? Were there more little chicks running around? While the chicks were cute, she had already been warned any excess roosters would be destined for the stew pot.

Even with a couple of hens trying to hatch babies, they were getting around several dozen eggs a day from the large flock. When the lodge was still operating, the chickens provided the eggs for meals. It was one of the Reynolds's advertising points, how they focused on farm-fresh meals—eggs from their own chickens and beef from a neighboring ranch. She'd told Kaelyn how they wanted to serve elk or venison they hunted but ran into issues with the health department. She even sold surplus eggs to the neighboring lodges.

Ruth had been preserving some of the eggs for winter by what she called water glassing. That was a process of mixing pickling lime and water before submerging the eggs in the solution. They already had two five-gallon buckets of water glassed eggs—about twenty-four dozen—and were working on a third bucket when they entered quarantine.

Only the cleanest eggs were used for water glassing since the eggs couldn't be washed prior to being submerged in the lime water. The eggs that weren't pristine were washed and used for their daily needs.

If they started having a surplus of eggs, Ruth would boil a batch and make pickled eggs with those. She assured Kaelyn that pickled eggs would be a welcome addition to a winter lunch, provided she could keep Dick out of them in the meantime.

Ruth had warned her that if the days got too hot, the laying would slow down, and as it would be during the winter, they'd have to ration their egg use. But while there was an abundance, they'd make the most of God's bounty.

Kaelyn fluffed her pillow, willing herself to relax, but sleep eluded her. The events of the past weeks played through her mind. The Star Bright attack, her grandparents' deaths, the isolation. It all seemed like a terrible nightmare, yet she knew it was all too real.

Preparing eggs and produce for winter also drove the realness home. She knew Ruth was concerned about when things would go back to normal. She'd told Kaelyn and Chloe they needed to be ready to hunker down for the long haul.

Chloe had stared past Ruth with a distant look, likely thinking about her family in Colorado and how to reach them. Kaelyn often wished she could be a better friend and help Chloe find a way home, but mostly, she feared she might actually leave. Despite their ten-year age gap, they had grown close, and she couldn't imagine the lodge without her.

She was about to give up on sleeping and go downstairs for some water when she heard a noise on the ladder. Kaelyn froze, now wide awake. It couldn't be Ruth. She never climbed up there at night and rarely during the day. And it wasn't Chloe, who was still sleeping soundly across the room.

The ladder creaked again, followed by the faint sound of boots scuffing against the floorboards. Someone was in the room. Kaelyn's breath caught as the air seemed to shift, the unmistakable presence of another person making her skin prickle.

Before she could process what was happening, rough hands grabbed her arms. She opened her mouth to scream, but a calloused palm clamped over it, muffling her cries. The smell of sweat and dirt filled her nostrils as she thrashed wildly, trying to break free.

Who is this? How did he get in? Where is Ruth? The questions spun through her head as she fought against her attacker's iron grip.

From across the loft, she heard Chloe's startled yelp, followed by the sounds of a struggle. "Let go of me!" Chloe cried out, her voice thick with fear and sleep.

Hearing her friend in distress sent a surge of desperate strength through Kaelyn. She bit down hard on the hand covering her mouth, tasting blood. The attacker cursed, loosening his grip just enough for her to wrench free.

Kaelyn opened her mouth to scream, but the sound barely escaped before something rough and damp was shoved between her teeth, cutting her off. She thrashed against the hands pinning her, muffled cries of terror escaping as her heart pounded wildly.

"Kaelyn!" Ruth's voice rang out from below, followed by the sound of something heavy hitting the floor. Was Ruth fighting back? Had she taken down one of the intruders?

Hope flared in Kaelyn's chest, only to be extinguished as strong arms wrapped around her waist and lifted her off the bed. She kicked and flailed, her elbow connecting with something solid. Her attacker grunted but didn't let go.

In the darkness, Kaelyn couldn't see who was holding her or how many intruders there were. She could hear Chloe still struggling, Ruth's muffled protests from downstairs, and the harsh breathing of the man restraining her.

They moved toward the ladder, Kaelyn fighting every step of the way. She dug her heels in and tried to grab onto anything within reach. She even hit him with her cast, but it was useless. Her bare feet slipped on the smooth floor, and her fingers found no purchase in the darkness.

As they reached the ladder, panic surged through her. How were they going to get her down? Would they throw her? The thought made her struggle even harder, twisting and turning in her captor's grasp.

She felt the sickening lurch as they began to descend, her stomach dropping as if she were on a roller coaster. The man holding her had one arm wrapped tightly around her waist, the other gripping the ladder. Kaelyn's feet dangled uselessly, occasionally brushing against the rungs.

Halfway down, Kaelyn's foot caught on a rung. For a moment, she thought she might have found some leverage, a way to break free. But instead, it threw her captor off balance. His grip loosened as he released a startled curse, and they were falling.

They tumbled the rest of the way down the ladder, a tangle of limbs and muffled cries. They hit the cabin floor with a heavy thud that knocked the wind out of her. Pain exploded across her back and shoulders. For a moment, she lay there, stars dancing in her vision.

She tried to call out for Ruth, to speak around the gag in her mouth, but the sound was garbled.

Ruth's angry voice cut through the chaos. "Get your hands off them, you— "

Her words were cut short by a dull thud, followed by Chloe's anguished cry. "Let me go!"

Fear gripped Kaelyn's heart. What had they done to Ruth? Was she hurt? Or worse? And what about Chloe? She tried to push herself up, to see what was happening, but her limbs felt like lead.

Before she could gather her strength, a fist gripped Kaelyn's hair, dragging her across the floor. She cried out in pain and clawed at the arm, trying to free herself, but the grip was unyielding. Her nails raked across skin, drawing blood, but her attacker didn't slow. He kept pulling her along.

The rough wooden floor scraped against her skin. In the dim light filtering through the windows, she caught glimpses of booted feet, dark clothing, and shadowy figures moving about the cabin. How many of them were there?

They entered Ruth's room, moonlight spilling through the window. It provided enough illumination for Kaelyn to see Ruth's bed was empty, the covers thrown back haphazardly.

"What's going on in there?" a man's gruff voice called from outside.

The one holding Kaelyn spoke in a low, urgent tone. "This one's a wildcat. Help me carry her before those guards decide to come in."

Carry her? Where were they planning to take her? She renewed her struggles, trying to twist out of her captor's grasp.

"I've got the other one," another voice replied from somewhere in the cabin. "She fell and knocked herself out."

Kaelyn's heart clenched. Chloe. Was she hurt? Had they hurt her baby?

"Leave her," said a third man who was closer to Kaelyn. His voice was cold, authoritative. "This is the one Bruce wants. The other was a bonus."

Bruce? Who is Bruce? And why does he want me? A flood of questions rushed through her head as she tried to make sense of what was happening. Was this about the Star Bright attack? Had someone found out she'd survived close contact with an infected person?

"What about the old lady?" someone asked, and Kaelyn recognized the voice of the man who'd first grabbed her in the loft. The reply sent a chill down her spine.

"Kill her for all I care. Let's go."

No! Kaelyn thought, renewing her struggles with desperate strength. They couldn't kill Ruth. She couldn't leave Chloe. This couldn't be happening.

They moved toward the courtyard door, Kaelyn still fighting weakly in her captor's grasp. Her bare feet dragged across the floor, catching on the uneven boards. She tried to dig her heels in, to slow their progress, but it was useless.

As they stepped into the courtyard, the sharp gravel dug into her feet, sending jolts of pain through her. The cool night air hit Kaelyn's skin, raising goosebumps. The stars above seemed to shine down on her, so peaceful and calm compared to the frenzy unfolding below.

A gunshot shattered the night, the sound echoing off the surrounding mountains. Kaelyn's blood ran cold. Ruth? Had they killed her? No, it couldn't be true. Ruth was tough, a survivor. She wouldn't go down without a fight.

A second shot followed almost immediately. Chloe? No, no, no. This couldn't be happening. Not Chloe and her unborn baby. They were innocent. They didn't deserve this.

"No!" Kaelyn murmured around the gag, her throat raw with fear and anguish. She had to do something. She had to get away, to help Ruth and Chloe if they were still alive.

"Get moving," her captor growled, his grip tightening painfully in her hair. "The guards are here."

Before she could react, something hard struck the side of her head. Pain exploded behind her eyes, and stars danced across her vision.

As consciousness slipped away, Kaelyn's last thoughts were of Ruth and Chloe. Had she imagined the gunshots? Were they still alive? She had to believe they were. She had to hold on to hope.

Then, everything went black.

Chapter 22

Kaelyn's head throbbed as consciousness slowly returned. The cold, damp stone beneath her was a stark reminder that the previous night's events hadn't been a nightmare. She was being held captive, bound and gagged in what appeared to be a cave. The air was heavy with the scent of earth and moisture, a far cry from the fresh mountain air she'd grown accustomed to at the lodge.

Her entire body ached, each small movement sending waves of pain through her muscles as her head pulsed. Her bare feet stung, raw and bloody from being dragged out of her bed and to God only knew where. The cast on her broken arm felt heavy and confining.

They'd managed to tie the ropes expertly around the cast and the wrist of her other arm. Each time she moved, the ropes seemed to tighten, digging into her skin. A deep chill had settled into her bones, making her shiver uncontrollably. The night clothes she wore, shorts and a tank top, offered little protection against the cave's damp coolness, and goosebumps rose on her exposed skin.

Blinking against the dim light, Kaelyn took stock of her surroundings. The cave was spacious, its rough walls disappearing into shadows that seemed to shift and move with a life of their own. A lantern flickered nearby, casting shadows that danced across the rocky surface. The orange glow did little to dispel the darkness pressing in from all sides.

Kaelyn shut her eyes, trying to figure out where she might be and hoping to calm the pounding in her head. The North Fork had several caves, though most were shallow rock shelters rather than true caves. This one seemed larger, more open. Where could she be? She took a steadying breath and opened her eyes.

She could make out at least six men moving about, their low voices echoing in the cavernous space. Their words were indistinct, but their tone was casual, almost bored. This was routine for them, Kaelyn realized with a chill. How many other people had they kidnapped?

As her eyes adjusted to the gloom, she noticed another girl, close to her own age, similarly bound and gagged. Their eyes met, and Kaelyn saw a mixture of fear and resignation in the other girl's gaze. She tried to communicate silently, raising her eyebrows in question, but the girl shook her head slightly, her shoulders slumping in defeat. The message was clear, don't bother trying to escape.

Kaelyn closed her eyes, trying to piece together what had happened. She had a vague memory of being in a truck, jostled and disoriented, the rumble of the engine vibrating through her body. But everything else was a blur of confusion and fear. Where were they? How far from the lodge had she been taken? And who was Bruce, the man they'd mentioned?

What about the gunshots she'd heard? Had they killed Ruth and Chloe? Tears filled her eyes as she struggled against the panic rising in her chest. The images of her friends in danger flashed through her mind, making it hard to breathe. *No, they can't be gone.*

The girl across from her jerked her head, eyes wide with alarm. She made a muffled sound through her gag and shook her head vigorously. Her gaze darted meaningfully toward the men nearby, before returning to Kaelyn. The message was clear. Stop crying, be quiet.

Kaelyn took a deep, shuddering breath and forced herself to swallow the sobs threatening to escape. She blinked rapidly, willing the tears away. The other girl's panic was contagious, and Kaelyn felt her own heart beating out of sync as she focused on controlling her emotions. She gave a small nod to the girl, silently communicating she understood the warning.

She again tested her bonds, wincing as the rough rope bit into her wrists. The fibers were coarse, digging into her skin with every movement. The gag in her mouth was uncomfortable and made it difficult to swallow. The taste of cloth and her own fear filled her mouth, threatening to make her gag.

Kaelyn closed her eyes, fighting against the wave of despair threatening to overwhelm her. She had to stay calm, had to think clearly if she was going to find a way out of this. With her limbs aching, her head throbbing, and fear gnawing at her insides, staying focused seemed impossible. Maybe a nap would help.

Sometime later, Kaelyn stirred at the sound of a noise, her eyes fluttering open. The memory of her situation crashed over her, and panic rose in her chest. She locked eyes with the other girl, whose steady gaze carried a clear warning. Taking a shaky breath, Kaelyn fought to stay calm.

Her muscles ached from being in one position for so long, and thirst clawed at her throat. She tried to focus on her surroundings, looking for anything that might help her escape. But the cave offered little in the way of hope. Rock walls, no visible exit, and her captors were always within sight.

Though they were a distance away, she studied each of the men in turn, trying to memorize their faces, their mannerisms. One was tall and lanky, with a scar running down the side of his face. Another was stocky and muscular, his arms covered in tattoos. The others blended together in her fear-addled mind, a blur of beards and dirty clothes.

The girl caught Kaelyn's attention again, shaking her head as if she knew what Kaelyn was thinking. Her eyes seemed to say, *Don't bother. There's no way out.* But Kaelyn refused to accept that. There had to be a way. She merely hadn't found it yet.

As the hours dragged on, Kaelyn's discomfort grew. Her bladder ached, and she wondered with growing dread how they expected her to relieve herself while bound like that. The thought of having to ask one of the men for help made her cheeks burn with humiliation.

The atmosphere in the cave shifted. The men straightened, their conversations dying away as footsteps approached. Kaelyn's heart raced as a new figure entered her field of vision.

He was tall and well-built, with salt-and-pepper hair and brown eyes. There was an air of authority about him that made Kaelyn's skin crawl.

He had to be Bruce. He moved with the confidence of a predator, his gaze sweeping over the cave before settling on Kaelyn.

To her surprise, he approached with a gentle smile. "Hello there," he said, his voice warm and friendly. "You must be thirsty. Let me help you with that."

He knelt beside Kaelyn and carefully lowered her gag. The sudden absence of the cloth in her mouth was both a relief and a new source of anxiety. She licked her dry lips, eyeing the water bottle in his hand warily.

He tipped the bottle toward her, letting her drink. The cool liquid was a blessed relief to her parched throat, and Kaelyn had to resist the urge to gulp it down greedily. She knew drinking too fast might make her sick, and the last thing she wanted was to vomit while bound and at the mercy of these men.

"There now," Bruce said, setting the bottle aside. "Is that better? Are your bindings too tight? We don't want to hurt you, you know."

Kaelyn swallowed hard, her mind whirling. This kindness was unexpected and unsettling. It didn't fit with the brutality of her kidnapping, or the terror of the gunshots she'd heard at the cabin. Was it all an act? Or was he truly deluded enough to think he was doing her a favor?

"Why am I here?" she managed to ask, her voice hoarse from disuse.

His look was almost paternal. It reminded Kaelyn of the way her father used to look at her when explaining something complicated, and the comparison made her stomach turn. "I saw what they were doing to you," he said gently. "Keeping you locked up. I knew that was no way for you to live."

Kaelyn's brow furrowed, confusion mingling with a spark of anger. Did he genuinely believe his actions were some kind of rescue? She glanced down at the ropes biting into her wrists, the angry red marks glaring against her skin. The ache in her arms and the sting from her bindings told a far different story than his soft tone.

"And this is?" she snapped, her voice cold as she jerked her chin toward her bound hands. "You call this freedom?"

"You've been secured for your own safety," Bruce explained patiently, as if talking to a child. "It's only temporary. We'll be moving on soon. We have one more jewel to collect."

He glanced at the other girl and smiled. "Ain't that right, Jade?"

The girl shook her head, murmuring something behind the gag, but kept her eyes lowered. Kaelyn wondered how long she'd been held captive.

"I know, I know," Bruce chuckled, reaching out to pat Jade's cheek. The girl flinched away from his touch. "You're not too fond of your new name, but I think it fits you perfectly. Those beautiful green eyes of yours, just like the gemstone."

He turned back to Kaelyn, studying her face intently. His gaze now made her skin crawl, and she had to resist the urge to turn away. "And you . . . you look like a Pearl." He paused, frowning slightly. "No, not quite right. You're not a Pearl. Ruby? Yes . . . that's better. Ruby suits you."

Her stomach twisted at the thought of being renamed like some sort of pet. "My name is Kaelyn," she said firmly, trying to inject some strength into her voice despite her fear.

Bruce's smile never wavered, but something cold flickered in his eyes. "Ruby is your name now. You'll get used to it, exactly like Jade has. It's better this way, trust me. A fresh start, a new family."

He leaned in closer, his voice taking on an excited edge. "Soon, we'll leave. The rest of the family is waiting for us at Lake Yellowstone Hotel. We have the most perfect setup. I know you'll be truly happy there."

Before Kaelyn could respond, he replaced her gag, his movements gentle but firm. She tried to pull away, but he held her still, tying the cloth securely behind her head. "It's okay," he murmured. "I know it's uncomfortable, but it's necessary for now. You'll see."

He moved to Jade next, helping her drink from the water bottle. The girl's eyes were dull and resigned as Bruce carefully replaced her gag. "There we go." He patted her shoulder. "Not much longer now, I promise. Someone will be in to help take you to the facilities soon."

With a final smile at both of them, he stood and walked away, disappearing into the shadows of the cave. Kaelyn watched him go, her mind reeling from the encounter. She'd expected a monster, someone visibly evil. But his gentle demeanor was almost more terrifying. How could someone who seemed so kind be capable of such cruelty?

Kaelyn tried to make sense of what he said. Family? Lake Yellowstone Hotel? And what did he mean by "one more jewel to collect"? Was there someone else from one of the lodges Bruce was after? Or was it someone else entirely?

She looked around the cave again, desperate for any clue as to their location. But the rocky walls offered no answers. She didn't even know how long she'd been unconscious while they brought her here. The vague memory of the truck ride was all she had to go on, and that wasn't much.

Kaelyn's gaze drifted back to the other girl. Jade. How long had she been here? What had happened to her? The resignation in her eyes spoke of a long captivity, of hope slowly eroded away. Kaelyn tried to imagine what Jade had been through, and her heart ached with sympathy and fear.

But Kaelyn refused to give up. She had to find a way back to the lodge, back to safety. Ruth and Chloe might still be alive. They might need her help. And what about her parents? They were still out there somewhere, probably worried sick about her. The thought of them somehow making it back to the States, searching for her, not knowing what had happened, brought tears to her eyes.

As the lantern flickered, Kaelyn renewed her efforts to loosen her bonds. She twisted her wrists, ignoring the pain as the rope scraped against her raw skin. There had to be a way to slip free, to create enough slack to work her hands out.

But even as she struggled, a small voice in the back of her mind whispered doubts. What if she couldn't get away? What if Bruce did take her to this "family" at Lake Yellowstone? What would happen to her? Would she end up like Jade, hollow-eyed and hopeless?

Kaelyn pushed the thoughts away, focusing instead on the rough rope around her wrists. She wouldn't give up. She couldn't. Somehow, someway, she would find a way out of the cave and back to the people who cared about her.

As time crawled by, Kaelyn's determination never wavered. She might be bound and gagged, trapped in a cave with no idea where she was, but her spirit remained unbroken. Whatever Bruce had planned, whatever this "family" was, she silently vowed she wouldn't become a part of it.

She was Kaelyn Fisher, not Ruby or any other name Bruce wanted to give her. And no matter what it took, she would find her way home. She thought of her grandparents, of the strength they'd always believed she possessed. She thought of her parents, hopefully safe and trying to figure out a way to return home to her.

Kaelyn closed her eyes, trying to picture the lodge, the mountains, the safety she'd begun to feel in the quarantine cabin. It seemed like a lifetime ago now, but she clung to the memory. She had to believe she'd escape the cave and feel the crisp mountain air on her face, hear the rush of the creek, help take care of the chickens and the garden. Even peel potatoes under Ruth's watchful gaze.

As exhaustion began to overtake her, Kaelyn's thoughts drifted to the mysterious Bruce. Who was he really? What drove a man to kidnap young women and create this twisted version of a "family"? There had to be more to the story, some reason behind his actions. Understanding him might be the key to escaping, but the thought of getting inside his head was almost as terrifying as her current situation.

The cave grew quieter as night fell, or at least Kaelyn assumed it was night. It was hard to tell time in the unchanging gloom of their prison. The men settled down to sleep, their snores echoing off the stone walls. Only one remained awake, keeping watch over the captives.

Kaelyn tried to stay alert, to watch for any opportunity, but her eyelids grew heavy. The events of the day, the fear, the stress, and her aching head had taken their toll. As she drifted off into an uneasy sleep, her last conscious thought was a prayer. For safety, for rescue, and for strength to endure whatever lay ahead.

In her dreams, Kaelyn ran through endless caves, Bruce's voice echoing behind her, calling her Ruby. She searched desperately for an exit, for a glimpse of the sky, but everywhere she turned, there was only more darkness. She woke with a start, heart pounding, only to find herself still bound in the cave.

But as the initial panic faded, she felt a spark of something she hadn't expected.

Anger.

Anger at Bruce for taking her, at the men who followed his orders, and at the unfairness of it all. And with the anger came a renewed determination. She wouldn't be Bruce's Ruby. She wouldn't become part of his twisted family.

No matter what it took, no matter how long it took, Kaelyn would find a way out. She would survive this, and she would make it back to the lodge. She'd take Jade with her. Bruce and his men had no idea who they were dealing with. Kaelyn Fisher was stronger than they knew, and she was ready to fight.

Chapter 23

Kaelyn's wrist burned as she worked at the ropes binding her hands. Hours of subtle twisting and pulling had left her skin raw, but she could feel the bindings loosening as she used the cast to help fray it.

Across the dimly lit cave, the other girl—the one Bruce had called Jade—caught Kaelyn's eye and gave a slight nod. Seeing what Kaelyn was doing changed things. With a resigned sigh, she'd shaken her head but started working her own ropes. She, too, had made progress.

The cave was quiet, save for the occasional snore from one of their captors. Kaelyn's eyes darted to the man on guard duty, slumped against the wall, his chin resting on his chest. This might be their chance.

She raised her eyebrows at Jade, tilting her head toward the cave entrance. The other girl's eyes widened, a mix of fear and hope flickering across her face. She shook her head slightly, gesturing with her chin toward the sleeping guard.

Frustration bubbled up in Kaelyn's chest. They needed to act now, while the men were asleep. But how could they communicate a plan with gags in their mouths and a guard who could wake at any moment?

As Kaelyn was about to attempt some kind of sign language, a sound from outside the cave made her freeze. At first, she thought she'd imagined it. A faint pop, like a car backfiring in the distance. Then came another. And another.

Gunshots.

The guard's head snapped up, alert. He scrambled to his feet, fumbling for the rifle leaning against the wall beside him. "Boss!" he hissed, moving toward a section of the cave Kaelyn couldn't see. "Boss, wake up!"

More shots rang out, closer now. Shouts echoed from outside, the words indistinct but the tone unmistakable. This was an attack.

Bruce emerged from the shadows, his face hard. "How many?" he snapped at the guard.

"I don't know," the man replied, his voice shaking. "It sounds like— "

His words were cut off by a deafening explosion shaking the entire cave. Dust and small rocks rained down from the ceiling. Kaelyn squeezed her eyes shut, her heart pounding so hard she thought it might burst from her chest.

When she opened them again, the cave was in a frenzy. The men were shouting, grabbing weapons, and taking up positions near the entrance. Bruce barked orders, his earlier calm demeanor replaced by cold efficiency.

"Protect my jewels!" he yelled over the din. "They're what they're after!"

Two men rushed over to where Kaelyn and Jade were bound. Rough hands grabbed Kaelyn and hauled her to her feet. She stumbled, her legs numb from sitting for so long, but the man's iron grip kept her upright.

"Move!" he growled, shoving her toward the back of the cave.

This could be their only chance to escape, but with her hands still bound and two armed men guarding them, the odds weren't good.

Another explosion rocked the cave, closer this time. The sound of gunfire was constant now, punctuated by shouts and screams. Smoke drifted in through the entrance, stinging Kaelyn's eyes.

A figure appeared in the cave mouth, silhouetted against the swirling smoke. The guards raised their weapons, but before they could fire, more shapes emerged from the haze. The cave erupted in a deafening exchange of gunfire.

Kaelyn was yanked backward, deeper into the cave. Her captor was using her as a shield, his arm wrapped tightly around her throat. She could barely breathe, the smoke and the man's grip making her dizzy.

"Stay back!" the man shouted. "I'll kill her!"

The gunfire stopped. Through the settling dust and smoke, Kaelyn could make out several figures advancing cautiously into the cave. Her heart leaped as she recognized one of them. Dick Reynolds.

"Let the girl go," Dick called out, his voice steady but filled with barely contained rage. "It's over. You've got nowhere to run."

Bruce's laugh echoed through the cave, a chilling sound devoid of humor. "You think I didn't plan for this? There are more of us than you know. Kill us, and others will come for the girls. They're too valuable."

"What are you talking about?" Dick demanded. "What do you want with them?"

"They're my jewels." Bruce smiled calmly. "Part of my family."

"You're insane," Dick spat. "Let them go, now, or we'll— "

His words were drowned out by a sudden, blood-curdling scream. Kaelyn turned her head as much as she could in her captor's grip, her eyes widening in horror at what she saw.

Jade was thrashing in her captor's arms, her eyes wild and unfocused. The man holding her stumbled backward, confusion written across his face. To Kaelyn's shock and terror, Jade began to sing.

It was muffled by her gag, but the melody was unmistakable. "Twinkle, Twinkle, Little Star." The same song the infected man had hummed in the doctor's office before he went on a shooting spree. The same song the busboy had hummed before somehow blowing up the Irma Hotel and Restaurant.

"No!" Bruce shouted, his voice filled with disbelief and rage. "She can't be. Not my Jade."

Everything happened at once. Jade's captor, panicking, shoved her away. She stumbled forward, still singing, her bound hands clawing at her gag. Dick and his men raised their weapons. Bruce lunged for Jade, his face a mask of desperate denial.

In the pandemonium, the grip on Kaelyn's throat relaxed. She threw her head back, feeling the satisfying crunch as her skull connected with her captor's nose. He howled in pain, his arms falling away.

Kaelyn didn't hesitate. She ran, ducking and weaving through the confusion. Gunshots rang out behind her, but she didn't look back. She had to get out, had to get away from Jade.

Strong arms wrapped around her, and she lashed out, kicking and thrashing.

"Kaelyn! Kaelyn, it's me!" Dick's voice cut through her panic. "You're safe now. It's over."

She went limp in his arms, the adrenaline draining from her body. Over Dick's shoulder, she could see the cave entrance. Bruce and his men lay motionless on the ground. And Jade.

Jade had also escaped, making it to the mouth of the cave before stopping. She now was curled up in the corner.

One of Dick's men approached her cautiously, his weapon trained on her still form.

"Is she . . ." Kaelyn couldn't finish the question.

Dick shook his head. "I don't know."

"Bruce? The others?"

"They're dead," someone else said.

"Let's get you out of here. Someone grab the other girl. Be careful of her. She might . . ." His voice trailed off. They all knew what she might do as a Star Bright.

As they emerged from the cave into the early morning light, Kaelyn blinked, momentarily blinded. The scene outside was one of controlled mayhem. Men and women in hunting camo moved purposefully around the area, securing weapons and checking bodies.

"Dick!" a familiar voice called out. She turned to see Ruth limping toward them. Her arm was in a sling, but she was alive.

"Ruth," Kaelyn breathed, relief washing over her. "You're okay."

Ruth's eyes were filled with tears as she reached them. "I'm glad you're okay. A little banged up but could be worse." She looked like she wanted to hug Kaelyn but held back.

"I'm okay," Kaelyn assured her, though she wasn't entirely sure if it was true. "What about Chloe? Is she— "

"She's fine," Ruth interrupted. "Also a bit banged up, but okay. She's back at the lodge. I wanted to come with them, make sure you were safe."

Dick cleared his throat. "We need to get Kaelyn checked out. And we need to decide what to do about the other girl."

"The other girl?" Ruth echoed.

Motioning toward the mouth of the cave, Dick said, "She was with Kaelyn, but she seems to be a Star Bright."

"She wasn't." Kaelyn shook her head as they watched a man carry out Jade. Even though her hands were still bound and her legs loosely tied, a second man had his pistol trained on her. Her eyes were wild looking, darting around. Seeing Kaelyn, she stopped and began making noises.

"Watch her!" someone yelled.

"Take off her gag," Kaelyn said, taking a step toward Jade.

Ruth put out her hand to stop her. "Stay back."

"She's trying to talk."

Dick looked at Ruth, who gave a nod. "Go ahead and lower the gag," Dick said. "Keep your weapons trained on her."

Jade licked her lips and cleared her throat. In a hoarse voice, she said, "Pretty good fake, huh?" She smiled and nodded.

"You were faking?" Kaelyn said, not holding back her laughter. "It was a good fake. Scary good."

Jade grinned. "Thanks. Figured it was our best shot at getting out of there alive."

Kaelyn's relief mingled with admiration for Jade's quick thinking. "You're amazing," she said, glancing at Ruth and Dick. "We have to help Jade."

All eyes traveled toward Jade. She gave a light shrug. "My name is Natasha. Everyone calls me Tasha."

"Where's your family?" Kaelyn asked gently.

Tasha's eyes filled with tears. "I don't know. I think . . . they may be dead. I haven't seen them since I was taken."

"How long ago were you captured?" Dick inquired, his brow furrowed with concern.

"Four or five days? I'm not sure exactly. The days kind of blurred together. It was hard to know anything in the cave."

Dick nodded. "We'll look for them. Can you tell us where you were when they captured you?"

Tasha took a deep breath, steadying herself. "We weren't too far from the East Entrance. We'd been camping in the backcountry when everything happened. We were hiking out and my mom twisted her ankle. We thought there'd be a ranger since we didn't make checkout time. We made camp and let my mom rest for an extra night. The next day, we took it slow. It took two days to get out of our backcountry camp, and we never saw anyone. When we finally made it back to our van, the place was deserted.

"We went to check out, and the rangers were gone. Everyone was gone. We picked up some news on the radio and realized what was happening. Used our phones to check the internet but we couldn't get online. Cell service in Yellowstone Park isn't great. It was already late, and we decided to stay the night in the park. One night stretched into weeks.

"Listening to the radio, we thought with everything going on, we were safest where there weren't any other people. We were able to salvage food from a few places. When those sources were emptied, my dad said we should head to Cody. We planned to stay there a few nights and decide what to do. That's when they caught us. Bruce and the others."

A heavy silence fell over the group as they absorbed Tasha's story. Kaelyn felt sympathy for the girl, yet dread at the thought of what might have happened to her parents.

Dick exchanged a look with Ruth before turning back to Tasha. "We'll send out a search party as soon as we can. For now, let's get you both to the lodge and have Daisy examine you properly."

The ride back to the lodge was a blur. Kaelyn's mind was reeling, trying to process everything that had happened. Tasha sat next to her, the girls grasping hands, each seeking comfort in the other's presence. Kaelyn could feel Tasha's hand trembling slightly, mirroring her own unease.

They sat in silence for a while, the hum of the vehicle providing a backdrop to their racing thoughts. Occasionally, they exchanged glances, eyes wide with unspoken understanding. She squeezed Tasha's hand tighter whenever a wave of anxiety washed over her.

"Are you okay?" Kaelyn finally whispered, her voice barely audible.

Tasha shook her head, tears welling up in her eyes. "I don't know. That was so scary."

Kaelyn nodded, her own eyes misting. "I know. But we're safe now."

From the front seat, Dick glanced back at them in the rearview mirror with a concerned expression. "You two holding up back there?"

Kaelyn managed a weak smile, grateful for the concern. "We're hanging in there," she replied, her voice steadier than she felt.

Tasha nodded, wiping away her tears and offering a small, appreciative smile.

The rest of the ride continued with only brief exchanges, each word a step toward regaining a sense of normalcy. As they approached the lodge, a glimmer of hope sparked inside Kaelyn, bolstered by the presence of Tasha and the support of those around them. Though now safe with Bruce and his men no longer able to hurt them or anyone else, Kaelyn still couldn't shake the feeling their ordeal was far from over.

Chapter 24

Relief flooded through Kaelyn at the sight of the lodge, but it was quickly followed by a surge of anxiety. The familiar building, once a symbol of hope and safety, now seemed fragile and exposed. Her eyes darted around, scanning the tree line for potential threats.

Stepping out of the vehicle, her legs trembled, partly from exhaustion and partly from fear this might all be a dream. She might wake up back in the dark, damp cave. The feel of gravel under her feet, the scent of pine in the air, the distant call of a bird—every sensation seemed almost painfully vivid after the sensory deprivation of her captivity.

A crowd had gathered near the entrance, faces both familiar and new, peering at her with a mix of concern, relief, and curiosity. Kaelyn felt self-conscious, aware of her disheveled appearance.

She was enveloped in a group hug that nearly knocked her over. The physical contact was almost overwhelming, and she found herself torn between wanting to lean into the comfort and the urge to pull away.

Chloe was there, sporting a nasty black eye but smiling through her tears. Behind her, Kaelyn could see Von and Daisy, their faces etched with worry and relief. Even people from the other two lodges that she'd only met briefly before her kidnapping were there, their presence a reminder of how everyone was working together. How they'd organized to save her.

The atmosphere was charged with a strange energy. Joy at her return mingled with an undercurrent of fear and tension. Kaelyn could sense the unasked questions hanging in the air. What had happened to her? Were they all still in danger? What new threats might be lurking just beyond their perimeter?

"Did they hurt you?" Chloe asked, her hands gently cupping Kaelyn's face.

"No, not much," Kaelyn replied, her voice shaky. "I'm okay."

But even as the words left her mouth, she wasn't sure if they were true. Physically, she might be mostly unharmed, but the emotional toll of her ordeal was only beginning to make itself known.

"Are you sure?" Daisy asked, looking intently into Kaelyn's eyes.

"I'm fine, really," she insisted. "Thanks to Dick and the others rescuing us, and Tasha's diversion—pretending to be a Star Bright and freaking everyone out."

Daisy's eyebrows shot up to her forehead. "Oh?"

Kaelyn took a minute to explain Tasha's ruse. "She was amazing."

Tasha, standing nearby, gave a timid wave. "I'm glad it worked. I wasn't sure if they'd buy it or not." Her voice was still rough, strained from having the gag in place for so long.

Chloe turned to Tasha. "That was incredibly brave of you. Thank you for helping Kaelyn."

Tasha shrugged, looking a bit uncomfortable with the attention. "I did what I had to do. We both wanted to get out of there."

As the initial excitement of the reunion died down, Kaelyn noticed two men she didn't recognize standing nearby. One was around Dick's age, with graying hair and kind eyes. The other was younger, probably in his late thirties or early forties.

Dick followed her gaze and gestured to the younger man. "Kaelyn, this is my son, Rich. He lived in Oregon before all this. And this is his friend, Jim Verley."

Rich stepped forward. "How are you holding up?"

Kaelyn shrugged, unsure how to answer. "I'm . . . I don't know. It's a lot to process."

Jim nodded sympathetically. "I can't even imagine. But you're safe now."

"For now," she muttered.

The others exchanged a look.

Kaelyn glanced at Ruth. "What?"

Ruth shook her head as Daisy said, "The violence is increasing. Star Brights aren't the only threat, as evidenced by your kidnapping."

"And the trouble we had getting here," Rich Reynolds added. "We were attacked only a couple of miles down the road." He motioned to a van parked at the edge of the lot. Most of the windows were missing, including the windshield, and there were obvious bullet holes in places. "My dad and his friends were out looking for you and came to our rescue."

"Attacked by who?" Tasha asked. "Bruce and his gang?"

Rich shrugged while Dick muttered something that sounded like idiots.

"We suspect they wanted our van," Jim Verley added.

Daisy shook her head. "Seems a shame to die over a beat-up van."

"We thought they may be part of the group that took Kaelyn," Dick said. "But now we're not so sure. Not after finding the cave and discovering how well-armed the captors were compared to the group on the road."

Jim and Rich exchanged a look. "I suppose we'd better get back to the others."

"Thank you for your help," Von stuck out his hand, shaking with each of the men.

Kaelyn caught Ruth's eye. "Rich and his family, those he arrived with, are in the quarantine cabin. We've increased security for all the cabins and tents so what happened to you won't happen to anyone else. We brought Jim and Rich out to help secure the lodge after the cave was found."

"Really?" Kaelyn asked with a gasp. "You weren't worried— "

"Most of the Star Brights are younger than us," Jim said. "People my age are rarely affected. People Rich's age not too often either. It was a calculated risk on their part."

"We prayed about it," Ruth said. "Prayed about what was best to do to get you home safely."

A silence fell over those gathered around. Dick cleared his throat. "We need to remember God is still in control, even in these dark times. We must trust in His plan."

Rich shook his head, his expression troubled. "It seems we're in the last days. I'm not even sure what we do now."

"We turn to Him," Dick replied firmly. "That's what the Bible tells us to do."

Kaelyn listened to their exchange, her mind whirling. She'd grown up in the church, believed in God and Christ, but the idea of these being the end times felt impossible. Part of her wanted to cling to her faith, to believe there was a greater purpose to all this suffering. But another part couldn't help but question why a loving God would allow such sadness and pain.

Before she could dwell on it further, Daisy spoke up. "I hate to say this, but Tasha needs to be examined and must go into quarantine. We can't risk exposure to the rest of the group."

"No, you can't lock her up," Kaelyn said. "Not after everything she's been through."

Dick turned to Tasha. "I'm truly sorry about what happened to you. But we also need to keep everyone safe. We don't know if you've been exposed."

"Kaelyn may need to return to quarantine too," Daisy added. "Did you come in contact with someone else's blood?"

"No, of course not. They barely touched me. They didn't even hardly come around us."

Dick turned to Rich and Jim. "Can you two handle that? Would you be willing to allow her to join you in your cabin?"

Rich nodded. "I'm sure that would be fine. Beth and Alyson will take care of her." He turned back to Tasha. "My wife Beth and daughter Alyson, she's only a few years older than you. My son Eddie is also in the cabin. He's thirteen. A few days ago, we picked up a little girl, Zoe. She's staying with us, as is Jim and our friend Eva."

Tasha's eyes widened in fear, and she turned to Kaelyn, silently pleading for support.

Kaelyn reached out and squeezed Tasha's hand. "It'll be okay. It's a precaution. I'll make sure they take good care of you."

Tasha nodded, visibly relaxing a little. "Okay. If you think it's necessary. But only . . ." She took a breath and whispered, "Only until they find my family. I'll want to be with them."

Kaelyn gave Tasha's hand another squeeze and nodded. Deep down, she doubted Tasha's parents would come to the lodge, but she clung to the hope she was wrong.

Daisy stepped forward, her expression sympathetic but firm. "Let's get you both checked out."

She ushered them into the lodge. Most of those gathered around dispersed, but Kaelyn noticed Dick and a few of the others stayed nearby. If Tasha truly was a Star Bright, they'd respond as needed. Both Ruth and Chloe stayed during the examination.

She examined them carefully, checking for injuries. After a thorough inspection, Daisy stepped back with a nod. "You're both banged up but otherwise seem physically healthy. I know the emotional toll of such an ordeal isn't something that is going to go away . . . not anytime soon."

Kaelyn's eyes filled with tears as she gave a nod.

"We'll be here for you," Chloe said, resting her hand on Kaelyn's shoulder. "For both of you."

"Thank you." Kaelyn's voice was hoarse. She cleared her throat. "Do I need to go back into quarantine?"

Daisy gave a slow shake of her head. "I don't know. For safety's sake, it seems you should. But none of those *men* had any symptoms, right?" She spat the word men and made a face.

"No symptoms," Kaelyn agreed. "No one was singing or humming. They didn't even come around us. Other than the night they took me, they stayed away. Bruce, the leader, he came to talk to us and one time one of the other men took me to use the . . . um . . . a tree. But that was it."

"Same," Tasha agreed, nodding her head. "I'm not a Star Bright. I was faking."

Giving her a sad smile, Daisy said, "I understand. But we don't know you. Kaelyn met you in the cave. We don't know if you've been exposed."

"How could I be exposed when the only people I saw, before I was kidnapped, were my family? When do you think they'll go look for them?" Tasha gestured toward Dick and Rich, who were talking quietly in the doorway.

"Soon," Ruth said. "We'll get you settled first, and after that, they'll talk with the others and make a plan to go out. We try not to venture too far from the lodges, for security reasons."

"But they will look for them, right? Can I go along?"

Daisy looked at Ruth, who shook her head. "It's better if you stay here. We'll get you settled into the quarantine cabin— "

"It's the same cabin Kaelyn, Ruth, and I were quarantined in," Chloe added with a smile. "You'll like it."

With the examination wrapped up, Kaelyn told Tasha she'd visit her as often as she could.

"They'll let you visit me while I'm in quarantine?"

"Through the window. We'll bring food and whatever you need, and we can talk. I don't know any of the people you'll be staying with, but I'm sure it'll be fine."

"And when they find my family?"

Kaelyn looked at Ruth. The expression on Ruth's face told her she doubted the family would be found. Not alive, anyway. But Ruth's voice was neutral when she said, "We have five quarantine areas set up. One of the tents is still empty. We'll put you and your family in there together."

Tasha smiled and let out a breath. When she looked at Kaelyn again, there was a sheen of tears in her eyes. "That would be nice. I miss them. Even my brother, who can be a major pain sometimes."

As Rich and Jim led Tasha away, a wave of exhaustion washed over Kaelyn. The adrenaline of the rescue and reunion was wearing off, leaving her drained and sore.

Ruth seemed to sense her fatigue. "Come on. Let's get you cleaned up and fed, and after that, you can rest. I suppose we can even let you skip your chores for today." Ruth gave Kaelyn an exaggerated wink.

Chapter 25

The day after her rescue, Kaelyn woke up feeling surprisingly refreshed. Despite the ordeal she'd been through, a good night's sleep in a safe, familiar bed had done wonders for her spirit.

She still had a slight throbbing between her eyes and the rope burns on her wrists hurt, but overall, she knew she was going to be okay. As she got dressed, she could hear the lodge coming to life around her—the clatter of pots and pans in the kitchen, muffled voices discussing the day's tasks.

When Kaelyn made her way downstairs, she found Ruth in the kitchen, packing up food for those in quarantine.

"Good morning," Ruth said, offering her version of a smile, the corners of her mouth barely lifting. "How are you feeling?"

"Better," she replied. "Can I help?"

Ruth nodded, gesturing to a stack of containers. "We're taking today's food to the folks in quarantine. Want to come along?"

Kaelyn agreed. She helped finish packing the food in containers and loaded it into the back of the UTV Ruth previously used for cleaning the cabins and delivering items to their guests. Chloe and a few others helped load, but only she and Ruth made the deliveries.

"Are you okay to drive with your arm?" Kaelyn asked.

"Sure. It's a sprain. Daisy has me wearing the sling as a precaution. The woman who arrived with my son, she's also a retired nurse. She checked me, too, before she went into quarantine. She agreed with Daisy's assessment."

"She's a nurse?"

"Yep. She worked in a small hospital on the Oregon coast before she retired. God is certainly looking over us. Daisy was relieved to meet the woman. Eva Samms is her name. We'll go to their cabin first."

Passing the guard shack, a hastily constructed lean-to that gave the guards a place to get out of the weather, Ruth waved to those on duty. From her time in quarantine, Kaelyn knew there'd be at least three on duty at all times.

Previously, one stayed in the shack while two walked the grounds on patrol. A small smile flitted across her face as she remembered the guards busting in on them when Chloe and she were arguing. Was Chloe still thinking about leaving? She hadn't said anything since Kaelyn returned to the lodge.

Ruth knocked on the door, announcing their presence, before calling out, "Rich? I've brought your food for the day."

They moved to the window nearest the door.

"Good morning, Mom," Rich said from the open window. "Let's move over to the bedroom area. Jim and I were thinking of something and wanted to run it by you."

"All right," Ruth agreed with a nod.

"I'm fine on my own," Kaelyn said.

Rich disappeared, and his face was replaced by that of a little girl. "Hi," she said shyly.

"Hello there," she replied, smiling. "I'm Kaelyn. What's your name?"

"Zoe," the girl answered. There was a pause, then she added, "I'm an orphan, you know."

The blunt statement caught Kaelyn off guard. "I'm sorry," she said softly. "I'm kind of an orphan too. My grandparents were taking care of me while my parents are out of the country. My grandma died first, and then my grandpa died a few days later. I don't know how my parents are doing or if they're alive. The phones don't work right now for me to reach them."

Zoe tilted her head, curiosity replacing some of the sadness in her eyes. "Where are they?"

"Africa," Kaelyn replied.

To her surprise, Zoe brightened at that. "They're probably okay. Mrs. Samms said this isn't a zoo disease, and Alyson said Africa doesn't have as many Star Brights."

Kaelyn blinked, confused. "Um, okay. What's a zoo disease?"

Zoe shrugged. "You should ask Mrs. Samms. She's a nurse and knows things." The little girl's face grew serious again. "My daddy was a Star Bright. That's how my mom and him died. We had to leave our house and hide in a truck where we couldn't talk. We had to be quiet. We got to a safe place and there was a car for us. We were going to Dakota where my mommy's parents lived. But when we were driving, my daddy started humming and my mom got scared. She told him to pull over, but he kept humming."

Kaelyn's heart ached for the little girl. Before she could think of what to say, Zoe continued. "Sometimes I hum, but I see that people get scared. I don't want to scare them, so I don't hum about stars. I hum about Jesus and how much he loves me. He loves you, too, you know."

Despite the heaviness of the conversation, Kaelyn felt a warmth spread through her chest at Zoe's words. "Yes, I do know. But thank you for reminding me."

After a moment, Kaelyn asked, "Is Tasha here? Can I speak to her?"

Zoe nodded and motioned for Kaelyn to step closer to the window. In a whisper, she said, "Tasha may be an orphan too. Do you know if they found her parents?"

She shook her head. "I haven't heard yet."

Zoe scooted away from the window, and a moment later, Tasha appeared. She looked tired but managed a small smile when she saw Kaelyn.

"How are you doing?" Kaelyn asked.

Tasha shrugged. "I'm okay. Waiting to hear about my family, though I think I know what they're going to tell me."

Kaelyn nodded sympathetically. "Hopefully it won't be long before we know for sure."

They chatted for a few more minutes before Ruth reappeared. "You about done with your visiting?"

Tasha stepped closer to the window. "I'll see you later?"

"Sure. I'll come back when I can. We have to deliver to the other people."

Kaelyn and Ruth got back into the UTV and moved on to the cabin next door. The woman and her daughter, whom Kaelyn had met from a distance while she was in quarantine, had only a few days left.

"Hello!" the woman said, her voice bright and cheery. "It's so good to see you. I heard about what happened. Are you okay?"

Kaelyn smiled, but a familiar worry rushed through her. Was she okay? She wanted to be, but the memory of being kidnapped and held in the cave threatened to again overcome her. She released a breath through her nose and widened her smile. "Did you know there's a little girl about the same age as your daughter staying next door?"

"Yes, we met them—well, you know, in the same way we met you. We only have a few more days here. After that . . ." She shrugged. "I'm not sure what happens."

"It'll be fine," Ruth assured her. "We've talked with the others, the people from the lodges we're working with. You'll be welcome to stay with us."

The woman let out a noisy sigh as tears filled her eyes. "Good. I'm so glad. I don't know what we'd do. When I heard about those men capturing people, I realized just how dangerous it would be for us. We're so lucky we didn't run into them before. Is it true they are holding people hostage at one of the Yellowstone hotels?"

Fear surged through Kaelyn again as Bruce's words echoed in her mind. He was collecting his jewels. She'd asked Tasha if she knew who the other girl was, but she had no idea. Where was she?

Kaelyn knew there was another group of survivors down the road, closer to Cody, from what Dick and Ruth had said. But they knew little about who was in that group. Was the other girl, the other jewel, there?

And how many people had Bruce already taken to the hotel? He called them his family. He mentioned women and children. Could Tasha's mother and younger brother be among them? If so, why wasn't Tasha taken there too? Why was she kept in the cave?

Too many questions and not enough answers.

Dick and Ruth had the same questions. Ruth had insisted they needed to do something about the people at the hotel in Yellowstone: rescue them from what was no doubt a prison. But Dick said it was too risky.

Besides, according to what they knew, Bruce was the leader of the group, and he was dead. Dick said it was highly likely the group would disband and those held would be fine. Ruth told him that was wishful thinking.

After saying goodbye to the woman, they delivered food to the two tents that held other people. Kaelyn didn't know any of them, and with the setup, conversations were different. Temporary fencing had been added at the front of the canvas outfitter's tents.

Ruth called out to the occupants as she reached the gate, letting them know about the delivery. A burly-looking man stepped out of the tent flap. "Thanks. We appreciate it."

Ruth waved and asked if they needed anything special. When he said they were fine, the two of them moved on to the next tent and repeated the process. The final tent was empty, so they headed back to the lodge.

Back at the lodge, Kaelyn asked Ruth what she could do to help. With a mischievous glint in her eye, Ruth assigned her to clean out the chicken coop.

"Really?" Kaelyn groaned, but there was no real annoyance behind it. After everything that had happened, even a smelly chore like that felt comfortingly normal.

Armed with a shovel, bucket, and fresh bedding, Kaelyn made her way to the coop. The chickens clucked and pecked around her feet as she worked, seemingly unbothered by the state of the world outside their little domain.

As she scooped out the old bedding, she found herself lost in thought. Zoe's words about her parents being okay in Africa had given her a glimmer of hope she hadn't realized she needed. Maybe they were all right. Maybe, someday, she'd see them again.

The repetitive work was almost meditative, and Kaelyn was so focused on her task that she almost missed the sound of a vehicle pulling up to the lodge. Curiosity piqued, she set down her shovel and walked around to the front of the building.

A group of men were climbing out of a truck, and with them were seven or eight people Kaelyn didn't recognize. They looked tired and disheveled, clearly having been through some kind of ordeal. Not a surprise in this broken world.

Dick, who hadn't gone out with the search party, came out of the lodge. "What's happening?" he asked, his tone cautious.

The man who seemed to be leading the search party stepped forward. "We found the van. The family was deceased. While we were burying them, a little girl came up and asked for help." He gestured to the group behind him.

Dick's face darkened. "And you brought them here? After all the troubles we've been having? Kaelyn kidnapped? My son and his family attacked just down the road?"

The search leader looked exasperated. "Look at them." He motioned toward the ragged group. "They've got children. No weapons."

"The people who attacked Rich did it with rocks and sticks," Dick countered.

The two men stared at each other for a long moment before the search leader spoke again. "Look, if you don't want them here, I'll take them to one of the other lodges. I only brought them here because of the quarantine rules, but they're staying."

"By whose authority?" Dick demanded.

"By what is right in God's sight," the man replied firmly. "You're a Christian, at least you claim to be. Act like one."

Dick bristled at that, but before he could respond, Ruth's voice called out from the porch. "He's right, Dick. Set them up in the empty quarantine tent. Let's at least give them a few good meals and see what happens next. Lord knows they need the food."

Dick didn't look happy, but he gave in. He assigned someone to get the new arrivals settled in one of the tents. The refugees seemed grateful, but Kaelyn overheard one of the women complaining.

"A tent? You have this house. Those cabins. You're putting us in a tent?"

The man with her tried to quiet her. "I'm sure it's temporary. You heard them— "

"Quarantine," the woman interrupted bitterly. "I heard. Like we're some kind of lepers."

As the group was taken toward the outfitter's tent, the woman's complaints faded into the distance. Kaelyn stood for a moment, watching them go, before turning back to her chore. Dick and Ruth remained in the yard, having a quiet conversation.

Only a few minutes passed when the sound of another vehicle made Kaelyn look up again.

"Goodness," she muttered to herself. "Crazy here today."

The van beeped its horn in an obvious rhythm. "Brian!" Ruth cried. "Dick! It's him. Brian's back."

"Are you sure?" Dick asked, his gaze not wavering as the van slowed to turn into the driveway of the lodge.

"Yes, the horn is the code he used to use to knock on our bedroom door. And look! His dirt bike is on the back of the van."

An arm reached out the driver's side window, waving. A tan SUV came into view, slowing to also take the turn.

"And that must be Heather," Ruth said. "It's Bea's SUV anyway, and as far as I know, she's still on the Alaskan cruise."

"Some cruise," Dick muttered as the vehicles pulled into the driveway and came to a stop.

Kaelyn's heart raced as she watched the scene unfold. Brian Reynolds, Dick's younger son, was back and he'd brought his family. Brian climbed out of the driver's seat of the van, and a boy who looked about thirteen hopped out of the passenger side. From the SUV emerged a woman—Brian's ex-wife, Kaelyn guessed—and a girl Kaelyn recognized from church last summer. Maddie.

Their eyes met across the yard, and Kaelyn's heart surged with relief. At least there was one familiar face in this crazy new world. Maddie gave her a small wave, which Kaelyn returned, grateful for the tiny moment of normalcy.

Ruth gave each of the children a hug and offered the woman a cordial nod. Dick's face lit up with relief at the sight of his son and grandchildren, safe and sound. His eyes darted between Brian and his family, a mixture of joy and concern evident in his expression. Kaelyn could see the tension in his shoulders ease slightly, even as new worries seemed to settle in.

After a brief, intense conversation with Brian, which Kaelyn couldn't quite hear, Dick started directing the family. Ruth joined them, her face mirroring Dick's relief. Kaelyn expected Dick to send them to quarantine, like all the other newcomers. But to her surprise, that didn't happen. Instead, Dick motioned toward the lodge, apparently inviting them inside.

Confused, Kaelyn edged closer, trying to catch what they were saying. As she approached, she heard Brian's voice, clear and urgent.

"Dad, we need to discuss how quarantine should work. It's not spread by blood or air," Brian said, his tone serious. "It's spread by playing a computer game."

Chapter 26

Kaelyn followed them into the lodge, trying to blend into the background but anxious to learn more. Others, including Daisy and Von, had gathered around. Chloe motioned for Kaelyn to go to where she was. When Kaelyn drew near, Chloe made a face. "You smell like the chicken coop."

"Sorry. Something is happening. Something big."

"Yeah. It seems so."

Brian looked around at the group that had gathered. "We know how it spreads, the Star Bright affliction. It's a video game. You know the one everyone was talking about— " He glanced toward his son. "Still talking about. It's probably a good thing the internet has been so spotty."

The woman with him, who had been introduced as Heather Reynolds, gave a nod. "Not spotty enough, though. We saw it with our own eyes. We were playing with a friend and . . . and he changed. Right then."

Resting a hand on her shoulder, Brian said, "I spoke with other people on my way to Casper to get Heather and the children. On the way back too. There are stories of people who go without the internet for days and still become Star Brights. We don't know how long it can take."

Daisy shook her head. "People don't get sick from playing video games."

"They do. They absolutely do," Heather insisted. "We saw it happen. Our neighbor, who was always nice to us, saw something in the video game and became someone else."

"Not possible," Daisy insisted. "He had to be exposed in some other way."

"As I said," Brian interjected, his voice firm, "I spoke with others who corroborated what Heather is telling you. I met a man in Shoshoni on the way to Casper. He said they knew a family that turned into Star Brights. He was at their house, having dinner. A group was playing the game, and one of them started talking about seeing something odd before ripping off his VR headset and singing a Bob Dylan song. One about a shooting star."

Daisy paled as she looked toward her husband. "The family from Billings— "

Von nodded. "They brought their gaming stuff. Said they figured it would help them pass the time."

Brian sighed. "Yep. When we found them, the mom had a VR headset near her. There were three other headsets on the floor by the television. At the time, we didn't know— "

"I don't understand." Daisy continued shaking her head. "Video games can't spread disease. They just can't. It's not possible."

"What if it's not a disease but some kind of mind control?" Brian asked. "Heather said her neighbor saw something none of the rest of them saw."

Kaelyn glanced at Maddie, who was staring at her shoes. The look on her face was a mix of guilt and fear, her eyes darting up occasionally as if she wanted to say something but couldn't bring herself to speak.

"So, anyone playing the game could be infected?" Ruth asked, her voice full of worry.

Brian gave a nod. "They could be, but we think . . . Heather and I have discussed this, and I stopped and talked with the man in Shoshoni on the way back. We think there's something in the game that not everyone sees. Those who do see it and click on it become Star Brights. At least that's the theory."

Ruth looked at her grandson. "You play the game, right? You and Eddie even play it together."

"We do, but I've never seen it, whatever it is. Tom, he was our neighbor, he said it was like sunshine. Maddie saw it, too, but she didn't click on it. Right, Maddie?"

Still staring at her shoes, Maddie gave a nod.

"I spoke with Rich this morning," Ruth continued. "Eddie brought his VR set with him, had it hanging off his backpack. This morning, Rich asked if we could figure out some way to get internet to the cabin, said it would help Eddie pass the time." Sadness crossed over Ruth's face. "He tried to play when they stopped in Clark, a little town near the Montana state line, but their internet wouldn't work."

Kaelyn had never played the popular video game, though she knew plenty of others who had. Video games weren't her thing. She preferred reading a book any day. While she shared some of Daisy's disbelief that sickness could be spread by a video game, she thought maybe Brian was right. Maybe it was some kind of mind control thing. People playing the game saw the sunshine and clicked on it. Clicking on it was somehow what changed them.

"I know Eddie's seen it before," Jackson said. "He's told me about it. But I'm not sure if he's clicked on it."

Dick and Von exchanged a glance. Von cleared his throat. "I'll head to the cabin, talk to Rich and find out what he knows. I'll ask if he's aware of the . . . what is it? A bouncing ball?"

"More like a bouncing sun," Jackson corrected. "Right, Maddie? That's what you saw?"

"If Eddie's seen it, he'll know," Maddie said confidently.

The room fell silent as everyone processed the information. Thoughts tumbled over each other as Kaelyn tried to piece it all together. If Eddie had seen the bouncing sun, then what? Did it automatically mean he would turn into a Star Bright? She remembered something.

"Wait," she said, her voice breaking the silence. "What about the people who became Star Brights but didn't play video games? Like the bus driver who drove into the river? He was old, my grandparents' age."

Brian nodded, acknowledging her question. "But we don't know he didn't play the game. While it's true, it's mostly teens and people in their twenties and thirties who became Star Brights, at least that's what the news focused on, anyone could play the game."

"Why haven't they told us?" Daisy's voice was high pitched. "You can't be the only ones to put this together. The CDC has been doing research. Surely they must know."

"We think they do." Brian shrugged. "One theory is that's why the internet is so spotty. They're trying to take it down."

"Whose theory?" Daisy asked.

"The man we spoke to in Shoshoni had a ham radio. Said there's been lots of chatter. They have a scientist who comes on sometimes. Someone who understands these things, who is working to solve it."

"We don't need a scientist," Daisy scoffed. "We need doctors."

"Doctors too." Brian nodded. "They had a team. But I don't think it's medical doctors who are needed as much as . . ." He glanced around the room. "Psychiatrists. They believe this is some kind of mind control thing."

Daisy shook her head. "No. That's not possible."

Heather Reynolds straightened her shoulders. "Do you know what MKUltra is? Operation Mockingbird?"

Daisy sent Heather a look Kaelyn couldn't quite interpret. "Those are conspiracy theorist fodder."

Heather crossed her arms. "You sure? I did some research on them after I first learned about them, and there is plenty of evidence to suggest they really happened. And now with this . . ." She made a wide circle with her arm. "Looks like they're back at it."

"You think the government is doing this?"

Heather shrugged while Brian shook his head. "Not necessarily. According to the man on the radio, the government is trying to keep the internet down."

"But it's not always down. Sometimes it works," Kaelyn offered. "I mean, I tried it this morning and got it to pull up on my phone. I emailed my parents."

Nodding, Brian said, "We've discussed that. What if— " He sighed. "You guys are really going to think I'm out there with this idea, but the guy on the radio thinks it's the game. The game is going in and making sure the internet goes back up."

"The game?" Daisy was shaking her head again.

"Maybe not the game, but the creators, whoever put in the mind control element."

"This reminds me of a movie . . ." Ruth said, touching her husband on the arm. "We watched it, remember, Dick?"

"What movie?"

"It's from years ago. A computer programmer has her identity stolen. She worked from home and found herself tangled up in this massive conspiracy. She has to go on the run, and it's all about how the internet can turn against you. It came out in the mid-1990s, right when the internet was starting to become a big deal, and it freaked people out. It made everyone think about how vulnerable we are online and what could happen if someone decided to take advantage of it."

"You have the movie on DVD," Brian said, gesturing toward the room holding the collection of old movies. "Maddie, Jackson, and I watched it last summer. Remember, kids?"

His daughter gave a barely there nod while his son looked thoughtful. "Maybe," Jackson said. "She went on vacation and this guy stole her passport?"

"Exactly. You laughed about how the game she was checking seemed so old. Even then, people were concerned about what the internet could do. And with the recent changes— "

"AI," Dick interrupted. "Artificial Intelligence. What if you're right? What if it's AI taking over the game and turning people into killing machines? It'd be like the Terminator movies. Instead of a nuclear holocaust happening, though, computers take over because all the humans are brainwashed to kill each other."

"I still find it hard to believe," Daisy said. "Computers aren't able to make people do crazy things. They aren't sentient beings. They can't think or feel or plan world annihilation. That's science fiction. The stuff of bad books and movies."

Maddie raised her chin. "I guess we're living in science fiction because this is actually happening. Tell them, Dad. Tell them what else the scientists said."

"Another speculation is . . ." Brian sighed. "Nanobots."

"Nanobots." Daisy scoffed. "Sure. Why not? That isn't any crazier than anything else you've said."

A chill ran down Kaelyn's spine as she looked around the room. The faces of those gathered reflected fear, disbelief, and determination. The revelation about the video game and its potential link to AI or even nanobots was both terrifying and, in a strange way, relieving. They finally had a possible explanation for the mayhem engulfing their world.

As the adults continued to discuss possibilities and theories, Kaelyn's mind wandered to her parents in Africa, to her friends back in Cody, to all the people she'd known and left behind. How many of them were at risk without even knowing it? The urge to warn them, to do something, anything, to help was overwhelming.

"At least if we know what's causing it," Brian said. "We can prevent it from affecting us here. It's easy enough to avoid the video game."

"But what about Eddie?" Jackson said, fear evident in his voice.

"We'll talk to him," his dad assured him. "We'll find out if he's seen the bouncing ball."

"And if he has?"

The room was silent as everyone considered the issue. If he'd seen it and clicked on it, then Eddie was the equivalent of a ticking bomb. The entire idea of it scared Kaelyn.

But as she caught Chloe's eye and saw the small, determined nod her friend gave her, Kaelyn realized Brian had brought back important news. They had information now, or at least the first pieces, but each revelation came with new obstacles. The world had changed in ways they were only beginning to understand, and the journey ahead would test them all.

Yet, as she looked around at their makeshift family—the Reynolds, the Weddles, Chloe, and the other survivors—hope flickered inside her. They would face this together, one day at a time. The road ahead would be difficult, fraught with dangers they couldn't even imagine yet. But they had each other, and now they had knowledge. It wasn't much, but it was a start.

And sometimes, Kaelyn thought, remembering her grandmother's words from that day in the doctor's office before their world fell apart, *a start was all you needed to change the world.*

Chapter 27

Over two months after Brian's return, Kaelyn stood by the window of the room she shared with Chloe in the main lodge, watching the sunrise paint the mountains gold and crimson. The crisp September air carried the scent of pine and wood smoke as the lodge prepared for winter.

Her cast had finally been removed, and though her arm was still weak, the freedom of movement was a daily joy.

Down below, Eddie and Jackson were at the woodpile. Their laughter drifted up to her, a sound that had become more common in recent days. Eddie's family had been released from quarantine after serving their two weeks. Their fears eased when Eddie confirmed he'd seen the bouncing sun in the game but had never clicked on it.

"It looked weird," he'd explained. "Like it wasn't supposed to be there. So, I just ignored it."

A simple decision he made months ago might have saved his life and the lives of others as well.

The rescue mission to Lake Yellowstone Hotel had been successful too. Dick and a team from all three lodges had freed twenty-three people—fifteen women and eight children—who'd been held captive as part of Bruce's "family."

Tasha had become close with one of the women from there. The woman had lost her daughter, and with Tasha losing her family, they bonded. Both had slowly begun to heal and found a place among the lodge community.

"There you are," Chloe said as she entered their room. Her belly was noticeably rounder now, the evidence of new life a reminder that even in darkness, hope persisted.

After weeks of uncertainty about whether to stay or attempt the dangerous journey to Colorado, she'd finally decided that the lodge was where she and her baby would be safest, at least for now.

"Ruth's looking for you. Something about checking the email again. She had a message come through."

Kaelyn's heart quickened. Every day since she'd been rescued from Bruce's cave, she checked her laptop, hoping for some word from her parents. The internet was unpredictable. Sometimes it worked for minutes, and other times it worked for hours before disappearing again. Most of the time, it didn't work at all.

During one of the rare connections, Maddie Reynolds had heard from her Grandma Bea, who'd been on an Alaskan cruise when the Star Bright trouble started. She was still in Alaska, living in an apartment. The town had worked hard to capture those affected, and there hadn't been any incidents in their small town for weeks. She was staying there for now, since it was safe, and would return to Wyoming when she could.

In the small office of the lodge, Ruth waited with the laptop open. "It's working," she said simply, stepping aside.

Kaelyn slid into the chair, and her fingers quickly navigated to her email. Her breath caught when she saw it—a new message, sent a week prior, with her mother's name beside it.

Dearest Kaelyn,

If you're receiving this, know that we are ALIVE. Communications from Africa have been nearly impossible. We've caught up on all your emails. Thank you for letting us know about your grandparents. Please know how much we wish we were there with you. We are eternally grateful to the Reynolds for keeping you safe.

The situation here is difficult but not as desperate as what you've described. We pray for all of you daily.

We've secured passage on a cargo ship that will leave as soon as it gets clearance. We hope that will happen in the next few days. It's a long journey home, but we're on our way.

Stay strong. Stay where you are. We will find you.

Remember what Grandma Joyce would say—God is making a way where there seems to be no way.

All our love,

Mom and Dad

Tears blurred Kaelyn's vision as Ruth's hand came to rest on her shoulder.

"They're alive," Kaelyn whispered. "They're coming home."

That evening, as everyone gathered for dinner, Dick stood to make an announcement. "Today, we received news that Kaelyn's parents are alive and making their way back to the States." A cheer went up around the tables. "And I want to share something that's been on my mind, something Terry Fisher and I had discussed when he first arrived."

He opened his Bible and read from Genesis—the same passage her grandpa had chosen when they were preparing to come up to the lodge. When he finished, Dick closed the book with care. "Jacob took his family to Egypt during a famine, not knowing what awaited them. They were strangers in a strange land, but they survived. They built a life. They became stronger."

He looked around at the gathered faces—some worn with grief, others bright with youth, all united by circumstance and choice. His gaze rested on Kaelyn. "Like Jacob, we didn't choose this journey. But here, in this place, we are becoming a family."

Once he looked away, Kaelyn glanced around the room at the people who had become her family in the absence of her parents and grandparents. Ruth with her gruff wisdom, Chloe with her quiet strength, Tasha rebuilding after terrible grief, the Reynolds and Weddles and all the others who had found their way to this sanctuary.

The world outside their mountain refuge was still broken. The Star Bright phenomenon continued, though less frequently now that the reason why it was happening was released. The scientist Brian had heard on the ham radio had managed to get his message out. There was new hope that they could stop it, even for those who had been exposed to the bouncing sun. If so, then maybe the nightmare would end.

No one knew if that would happen. Not yet, anyway. But here, in this place, they had found something worth fighting for.

A community, a purpose, a future.

As Kaelyn bowed her head for the blessing, she thought of her grandparents. They had known, somehow, that this place would be her refuge. Like Jacob, they had followed God's guidance into the unknown, trusting that what awaited was better than what they left behind. Now it was her turn to carry that trust forward, and help make this place home.

Thank you for spending your time on our new Star Bright adventure.

If you have five minutes, you'd make this writer very happy if you could write a short review on Amazon, Goodreads, Bookbub, or your favorite review site.

I appreciate you!

Join my reader's club!
As part of my reader's club, you'll be the first to know about new releases and specials. I also share info on books I'm reading, preparedness tips, and more.

Please sign up on my website:
MillieCopper.com/Freebie

Also by Millie Copper

The Havoc in Wyoming Series

When a series of coordinated attacks devastate the United States, the people of Bakerville, Wyoming, must come together to survive. Unfortunately, not everyone has the town's best interest at heart. Some are striving for personal gain during the apocalypse.

The Montana Mayhem Series

A group from Bakerville, Wyoming strikes out on their own while searching for the desires of their heart. Unfortunately, the road will not be easy, and sometimes the heart is hardened and deceitful. When things don't work out as they hoped, will they become stranded in the wilderness? Or will each be able to find their way home?

The Dakota Destruction Series

After a series of coordinated attacks devastate the United States, Katie and Leo sacrifice everything to help their country. But some things aren't as they seem. Is it time to go home and start fresh, or can something good come out of this terrible situation?

In The October Fall World

In the blink of an eye, an EMP changed everything for Lauren and her family. Now they are in a fight for survival, trying to keep their loved ones alive as society collapses around them. Their once peaceful town of Cody, Wyoming has turned into a powder keg. And with law enforcement a thing of the past, evil lurks around every corner.

Nonfiction Books

Millie has penned seven nonfiction, traditional food focused books, sharing how, with a little creativity, anyone can transition to a real foods diet without overwhelming their food budget. Many of her books also include preparedness and food storage tips.

Find these titles at:
MillieCopper.com

Acknowledgments

Thanks to:

Ameryn Tucker, my editor, beta reader, and daughter wrapped in one. I had a story I wanted to tell, and Ameryn encouraged me and helped me bring it to life.

Dee from Dauntless Cover Design.

My husband, who gave me the time and space I needed to complete this dream and was very patient as I'd tell him the same plot ideas over and over and over.

Three more adult daughters and a young son, who willingly listen to me drone on and on about storylines and ideas while encouraging me to "keep going."

My amazing Beta Readers! Thanks to Barbara, Christine, Cristy, Ilona, Linda, Melonie, Tammy, and Tracy for your help in creating the final story. Your insights and abilities to see the things I miss are very much appreciated!

And also, a special thank you to Tim, a specialist in all things that go boom, for always answering my questions and pointing out things I wouldn't even think about.

And to you, my readers, for spending your time on our new Star Bright adventure. If you have five minutes, you'd make this writer very happy if you could leave a review. I appreciate you!

About the Author

Millie Copper, writer of Cozy Apocalyptic Fiction and preparedness mentor, was born in Nebraska but never lived there. Her parents fully embraced wanderlust and moved regularly, giving her an advantage of being from nowhere and everywhere.

Millie Copper lives in the wilds of Wyoming with her husband and young son, tending chickens and attempting a food forest on their small homestead. After living off the grid for several years, they've recently gone back on the grid. Four adult daughters, three sons-in-law, and six grandchildren round out the family.

Since 2009, Millie has authored articles on traditional foods, alternative health, homesteading, and preparedness-many times all within the same piece. Millie has penned seven nonfiction, traditional food focused books, sharing how, with a little creativity, anyone can transition to a real foods diet without overwhelming their food budget.

The *Havoc in Wyoming, Montana Mayhem, Dakota Destruction, Wyoming Fall, and Yellowstone County Fall* Christian Post-Apocalyptic fiction series use her homesteading, off-the-grid, and preparedness lifestyle as a guide. The adventures continue with the *Lights of the Collapse* series.

Find Millie at www.MillieCopper.com
Facebook: www.facebook.com/MillieCopperAuthor/
Amazon: www.amazon.com/author/milliecopper

BookBub: https://www.bookbub.com/authors/millie-copper
Instagram: https://www.instagram.com/cozyapoc
YouTube: https://milliecopper.com/Youtube